I wanted Evvie to leave Miss Hattie's. I begged her to. "How am I going to feed my family?" she'd snap back.

"I'll help," I'd say lamely.

She'd laugh. "Yeah, sure. How do you propose to do that? You can barely afford to pay your rooming-house rent."

That hurt.

"You probably have to borrow the two bucks from Zeke to come here and see me," she added.

Now, that was hitting below the belt. It was doubly humiliating because it was true.

"Don't tell me you'll get another job. If there were other jobs available, you'd have one." Then she'd soften. "If I could do something else, Edgar honey, I would. If there was any other work out there, I'd take it. But I've looked. There isn't. Not for you and not for me…"

Dear Reader,

I was absolutely delighted when I learned that Harlequin Books was starting a new series about love that withstands the tests of time, place and circumstance—Everlasting Love. I was especially intrigued by the possibilities of using the era of the Great Depression and World War II as the backdrop for such a story.

It just so happens there really is a Miss Hattie's Bordello in San Angelo, Texas. A museum now, it operated as a "gentleman's club" for roughly the first half of the twentieth century and remained locked up, ignored, all but forgotten, for most of the second. I received my first tour of it several years ago when Mark Priest, its current owner, bought it.

The place is fascinating. Rooms have been named after Miss Kitty, Miss Blue, Miss Rosie, Miss Mable and Miss Goldie. But who were these women? What were their backgrounds? How long did they work there? What happened to them after they left? Intriguing questions, for which we have no factual answers.

Some things in Miss Hattie's will make you shake your head, smile, even laugh, but the dominant mood for me was one of haunting sadness. That long, narrow upper floor may once have been a den of pleasure, but I doubt it was ever a place of joy.

By the way, you won't find a room named after Miss Evvie. She's pure fiction, as are the others I mention in this book.

Today Legend Jewelers occupies the space that was once a dry-goods store. Mark Priest, its proprietor, has generously donated a necklace similar to the one in my story to be given to one of my readers. I hope you'll visit my Web site, www.kncasper.com, browse and enter the draw.

I enjoy hearing from readers. You can e-mail me at kncasper@kncasper.com or write me at P.O. Box 61511, San Angelo, TX 76906.

Ken Casper

Upstairs at Miss Hattie's

KEN CASPER

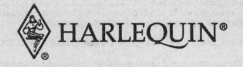

HARLEQUIN®

TORONTO • NEW YORK • LONDON
AMSTERDAM • PARIS • SYDNEY • HAMBURG
STOCKHOLM • ATHENS • TOKYO • MILAN • MADRID
PRAGUE • WARSAW • BUDAPEST • AUCKLAND

ISBN-13: 978-0-373-65417-8
ISBN-10:   0-373-65417-0

UPSTAIRS AT MISS HATTIE'S

ABOUT THE AUTHOR

Ken Casper, aka K.N. Casper, figures his writing career started back in the sixth grade when a teacher ordered him to write a "theme" explaining his misbehavior over the previous semester. To his teacher's chagrin, he enjoyed stringing just the right words together to justify his less than stellar performance. That's not to say he's been telling tall tales to get out of scrapes ever since, but…

Born and raised in New York City, Ken is now a transplanted Texan. He and Mary, his wife of more than thirty years, own a horse farm in San Angelo. Along with looking after their two dogs, six cats and eight horses—at last count!—they board and breed horses and Mary teaches English riding. She's a therapeutic riding instructor for the handicapped, as well.

Life is never dull. Their two granddaughters visit several times a year and feel right at home with the Casper menagerie. Grandpa and Mimi do everything they can to make sure their visits will be lifelong fond memories. After all, isn't that what grandparents are for?

Books by Ken Casper

HARLEQUIN SUPERROMANCE

HARLEQUIN NASCAR

★Home on the Ranch
★★The First Family of Texas

To Mary, who urged and encouraged
To Paula Eykelhof, who saw the potential
To Beverley Sotolov, who made it happen
and
To Mark Priest, the only brothel owner I know
Thank you all

In memory of Vera Koth
Who never had any doubts

Chapter 1

"Why are you pushing him away, my dear? I've watched the two of you together. I'm sure you love him."

Sarah Clyburn gave her husband Bram's grandmother a sharp, hurt look. "I do love him," she answered, then sighed. "More than I ever thought I could. More than I deserve. That's why I have to let him go."

Evvie sympathized. She understood the young woman's dilemma far better than Sarah realized. She, too, had thought about walking away.

"Sacrifice may seem noble, but it doesn't always bring the results we hope for. Sometimes it only makes victims of both parties." She studied the pretty but sad face. "You know he loves you."

Sarah closed her eyes and took a deep breath. "He doesn't always say the words, but he shows me in a million different ways. All I want is for him to be happy."

"How can you possibly imagine that leaving him will make him happy?"

They were sitting on the ranch house patio. Just the two of them. The heat of the Texas summer was past, the air now cool and refreshing, spiced with a hint of late-blooming sage. The view to the south was one of gently rolling ochre hills, freckled with dark green stands of oak and cedar under a cloudless blue sky. In the distance, cattle grazed contentedly.

Normally Evvie found the bucolic setting soothing, a sharp contrast in these, her mature years, to the turbulence of her youth, but today the peacefulness of the sepia landscape failed to resonate in her soul.

Bram Clyburn had married Sarah Wingate last spring on this very spot, a lovely June wedding. Evvie and Edgar had been delighted with the girl from the first time they'd met her, and they were happy to welcome her into the family.

Returning only a few days ago from a three-month-long Pacific cruise, they were shocked to learn the couple was now contemplating divorce. All because of a telephone call.

It apparently began when Bram managed to convince the San Angelo City Council to revise the current budget to accommodate the downtown redevelopment project without raising taxes. In Evvie's estimation, talking politicians out of a tax increase was akin to talking a horse out of drinking at a watering hole. Mayor Roy Dollfus, who also happened to be Bram's best friend from high school, apparently felt the same way, because he started floating Bram's name as a possible candidate to replace Millard Spicer, the incumbent state senator, whose three-term tenure in Austin was riddled with charges of corruption and campaign finance violations.

The prospect of such a challenge had prompted a call from Jane Spicer, the senator's wife, to Sarah, threatening to expose her *sordid past* if Bram persisted in opposing him.

"I understand Bram was aware of your background when he married you," Evvie noted. Until two days ago she and Edgar hadn't been, however, and the revelation that Sarah had been an "escort" during her college days had come as quite a jolt.

"I told him before he even proposed. I was so ashamed, Evvie. I was sure he'd leave me, but he insisted it was all in the past, that it didn't make any difference in the way we felt about each other…that he loved me for who I am in spite of what I'd done." A tear slipped from her brimming brown eyes. "We thought we could keep it secret."

"Some secrets are hard to keep, my dear."

"Exactly," Sarah agreed. "My past will never go away. It'll always be there, if not staring me and Bram in the face, then lurking in the background, waiting to ambush us. No matter what I do or say for the rest of my life, I'll always be a call girl, a hustler who sold herself for money."

She lowered her head. When she raised it again, her cheeks were wet with tears. "I'm not proud of what I did, Evvie." She paused and bit her lip. "And I'd never do anything like that again, but that's not the point. Bram has an opportunity to go places, to do things, but he won't even get a chance to with me as his wife, not with my past."

Evvie studied the downhearted girl and suppressed a smile. A past that wouldn't go away. It all seemed so overwhelming when you were young. If only Sarah knew...

"Don't you see?" Sarah continued in frustration. "Politics isn't the issue. No matter what he wants to do, my past will always be there, holding him back. How will people ever be able to respect him when they find out his wife was a prostitute? I can't do that to him, Evvie. I can't. It wouldn't be fair. He deserves to be free to do his best, to climb as high as he can go. He won't be able to do that with me dragging him down. He deserves somebody who can help him—"

"You think the only solution is for you to leave him?"

Sarah looked away. "He'll get over me." Her voice thickened. "He'll find someone else, someone worthy of him."

How much did the politician's wife really know? And how far was she willing to go?

Evvie was getting ready to ask how Jane Spicer had learned of Sarah's background but stopped when two men came into view.

She had no doubt where Bram got his good looks. Edgar Clyburn was broad shouldered and unbent despite his eighty-six years. She remembered when he could match his grandson's impressive physical strength and stamina, too. They both had full heads of hair. Edgar's was snow white now, while Bram's was dark brown, nearly as black as his grandfather's had once been. Most striking, though, were their eyes. Age hadn't dimmed the cerulean blueness of Edgar's, or the glint of humor that seemed to be an inherent part of them. Bram's were perhaps a bit more serious and more blue-green, the latter color probably inherited from her, but they were every bit as compelling and warm.

"I was wondering where you two had run off to," Evvie commented to her husband. She and Edgar had had time for only one brief exchange in the kitchen before lunch and had agreed on what they had to do, but they hadn't had time to work out the details of a plan.

"We were over by the corral," Bram said, "checking out your new colt. Daedulus is coming along fine. A real beauty."

Edgar gripped the arms of his wife's chair as he leaned over and kissed her on the forehead. Straightening, he added, "Bram's been telling me more about this high-class venture he's working on. He's advancing the Clyburn name to new heights."

Recognizing the housing shortage spawned by the depression and the Second World War, Edgar had launched Clyburn Construction in 1946 to build low-cost homes. Returning GIs eager to settle down and start families had bought them in droves. Thirty years later, their eldest son, Hank, had expanded the business by creating Clyburn Homes, a middle-income housing division. Now Hank's son, who'd earned a double degree in engineering and architecture at Stanford, was inaugurating another new project, Clyburn Estates, this one for high-dollar residences.

"Impressive designs," Edgar added proudly. "The country-club crowd is going to be living in the lap of luxury."

"I had a suspicion all those books his father bought him would pay off one day," Evvie said with a fond twinkle in her eye.

"Is there something you needed us for, Gram?" Bram asked, standing beside Sarah's chair. He'd offered his hand, and she'd clutched it, hardly the actions of two people on the brink of divorce.

"I was hoping you gents might be fixing to go into town." Evvie gazed steadily at her husband. "I was telling Sarah about the delightful sweetshop we found in Fukuoka, Japan. You remember it, dear. It got my mouth watering for the wonderful pecan fudge they have at Eggemeyer's. Sarah said she's never tried it, so… I thought if you two were in the neighborhood—" forehead slightly arched, she smiled up at him, pausing a moment to make sure eye contact "—maybe you could stop off and pick us up a sample."

"Fudge?" Bram stared down at his wife, his brow furrowed. "I thought you didn't care for fudge, that it's too sweet."

"I, um…" Sarah stammered, not sure what to say. This was the first she'd heard of fudge, too.

"As a matter of fact," Edgar piped up, coming to the young woman's rescue, "I have to restock our wine supply. I propose a Texas Merlot with our steaks tonight, if that's all right."

"Sounds perfect," Evvie said with a pleased smile. "Take your time, dear. I'm sure you boys have plenty to talk about. We have hours yet before dinner."

Bram shook his head, at a complete loss. When he and Sarah accepted his grandparents' last-minute invitation to the ranch for lunch, he'd expected a lengthy discussion of their dilemma. In truth, he'd been hoping his grandparents might have some wisdom they could impart that would resolve the crisis. But the folks had listened without comment to Sarah's recitation of the situation, then they'd served a leisurely lunch while regaling them with hilarious stories about the exciting places they'd visited and the exotic foods they'd eaten on their Asian trip. Through all the laughter, everybody had ignored the elephant in the room.

Okay, that was a warm-up—or a softening up—Bram had decided. With the meal out of the way, they'd settle down to a heart-to-heart chat about the current state of affairs. Except now his grandmother was sending him and his grandfather off on a fool's errand. Whatever she had up her sleeve, Gramps seemed to catch on and was playing along. Considering the number of years the two of them had been married, that shouldn't surprise him. At times he wondered if they even had to use words to exchange ideas. He hoped he and Sarah were headed for that same kind of lifelong commitment and unconditional devotion, until...

His own parents had never found it. They hadn't bickered or fought. They hadn't divorced, but when his mother died of cancer ten years ago, she left her grieving family with the sad feeling that she'd never been truly happy. Bram had asked his grandfather once if he knew why. The old man's enigmatic reply was that she'd never been blessed with hard times. It sounded crazy, but Bram thought he understood what Gramps meant. Marla James Clyburn had grown up pampered by her parents, then gone on to marry a man who'd continued to give her everything she could reasonably ask for. Bram wondered if she'd ever figured out the source of her discontent.

"Pecan fudge," he muttered now, following his grandfather's lead. "Any other kind?"

"Well," Sarah drawled, the smile on her face failing to hide her uneasiness, "while you're at it, why don't you see if they have any divinity. That would be delicious, too."

The men left and for a minute the only sounds were of birds twittering and Bram's diesel pickup grumbling out of the gravel driveway.

"Now, my dear," Evvie said, rising slowly, "why don't you finish clearing the table while I get the bottle of Cherry Herring I've been hoarding. I have a story I want to tell you."

Chapter 2

"Okay," Bram said as he turned off Clyburn Ranch Road onto the main highway into town, "I've figured out that Gram wants to talk to Sarah in private, but why didn't she just say that? What's all this nonsense about fudge? I've never known her to be interested in sweets and Sarah doesn't even like the stuff."

"Feminine wiles, my boy. Feminine wiles."

Edgar wasn't exactly sure himself what his wife of sixty-five years had in mind, but he'd learned a long time ago to go along when she gave him that look.

"You better get used to it, son. It's their chief weapon against us poor devils."

"Seems to me it would have been a lot easier to just tell us to get lost so they could talk."

Edgar laughed. "My, you do have a lot to learn about women."

He glanced over at his grandson. He was proud of the boy. Bram had a sharp mind and a quick wit, as well as a sense of responsibility and integrity. A sense of humor, too. At the moment, though, he was scared stiff and rightly so. Edgar didn't doubt for a second that the boy loved Sarah. It shone in his eyes every time he looked at her.

"Talk to me about what's going on, son. You never told your grandmother and me that Sarah had a shady past."

"Because it was none of your business. A man doesn't go around bragging to people that his wife used to turn tricks for fun and profit." Bram heaved a deep breath, flexed his fingers and curled them again around the steering wheel. "Sorry, Gramps, I didn't mean to take it out on you. It's just…everything's such a mess, and I don't know what to do about it."

Edgar waved the rudeness aside. Until he had more information he wouldn't be able to impart the aged wisdom his grandson probably expected from him.

"How did she get involved in this business to begin with? Do you know?"

"It started out as a dare at a sorority party," Bram explained. "Tease a particular guy to see how much he was willing to pay for sex. Except it went beyond teasing. She'd been drinking, more than she should have, and when it was time to say stop, she didn't. She was stunned when she woke up the next morning and found he had left the cash payment he'd promised."

"And that was the beginning," Edgar observed.

"It wasn't supposed to be, but it was," Bram acknowledged. He kept his eyes forward, focused on the road, though there wasn't a car in sight. "One of her sorority sisters told her a few days later that a friend of the man Sarah had been with had called and was willing to pay the same amount for her company. At first she said no."

"But the money was too good."

Bram nodded. "She'd obtained several student loans and was working part-time as a salesclerk in a department store in addition to carrying a full class load. She wasn't starving, but the prospect of making as much on one Saturday night as she did in two or three weeks at her regular job was hard to resist." He hastened to add, "It's not like she was doing it every night or leaning into cars windows on the street."

"When you met her—" Edgar started.

"She'd already graduated from college, moved away and was working in the accounting office of the logging company I hired on with every summer."

"She was no longer—"

"No, no." Bram shook his head. "That ended before she left school."

They drove in silence for a few minutes.

"When did she tell you all this?" Edgar asked.

"We started dating the summer before my last year in graduate school. It was getting increasingly apparent that we were interested in more than just…dating. I'd made a few sounds about marriage, but I hadn't actually proposed yet. We were spending the weekend hiking in the Sierras, when she told me. She said I deserved to know, and if I didn't want to continue our relationship, she understood."

Bram removed his foot from the accelerator as they approached a flashing yellow-lighted intersection, but there was no one around, so he stepped on the gas again and kept going.

"I was shocked, of course, and I have to admit I considered walking away. What man wants to hear his woman's been screwing other guys?" The bitterness of the comment was contradicted by the tenderness with which he added, "But I love her, Gramps."

Bram shook his head. "What she did was a mistake, and I wish to God she'd never done it, but…" He let the words trail off.

"This all took place in California?" Edgar asked.

"She'd just finished up at Berkeley when I entered graduate school at Stanford."

"How does the senator's wife here know about her…history?"

Bram huffed out a breath, clearly wishing the subject would go away.

"There was a big scandal out there toward the end of her senior year," he said. "It made national headlines. Her sorority got busted for pandering, and Sarah's name was on the list of so-called escorts who made themselves available."

He cautiously pulled out and passed a slow-moving

farm tractor towing a module of newly picked cotton on its way to the gin.

"I know what you're thinking, Gramps. That maybe she didn't quit—she just got caught. But by then she'd already stopped accepting appointments. Fortunately no formal charges were ever brought, but somehow the names of the girls got released to the press. That's probably how the senator's wife found out about her. If the newspaper hadn't published them, nobody would be the wiser, and we wouldn't be having this problem."

"We can never completely escape our yesterdays, son. They're what make us who we are today."

"Once a whore, always a whore, huh?" Bram posited sarcastically. "Is that it?"

"I didn't say that, son."

Bram groaned in frustration and cast his grandfather another apologetic glance. After Bram had had a couple of minutes to calm down, Edgar asked, "How do you feel about going into politics? Do you want to be a state senator?"

"Roy Dollfus says I'm a shoo-in, that I have all the credentials to unseat Spicer, who may soon be facing criminal charges for conspiracy and money laundering concerning his campaign financing. Roy seems to think I could even have a shot at the governor's mansion one day. Needless to say, he's unaware of Sarah's...background. At least, so far."

"You haven't answered my question, son. Do you want to go into politics or don't you?"

Bram shrugged. "The truth is I don't know. It's flattering to be asked, but I like what I'm doing now, designing houses. It's what I was trained for. This new project we're working on... Well, I've told you my ideas, my plans, the possibilities I anticipate. I wouldn't be able to stay involved with it if I had to spend all my time in Austin or on the rubber-chicken circuit, raising funds for my next campaign."

Edgar chuckled. "I served on the city council for one term years ago. No rubber chicken, but I didn't find the overall experience very pleasant or satisfying. Dirty business, politics. Never ran for office again."

Bram cruised past a car being driven on the wide shoulder of the road by an old man who appeared perfectly content to putter along twenty miles an hour below the speed limit.

"Somebody has to do it," he observed.

"No question about that, my boy, and I admire those who can handle the allure of power and still hold on to their integrity. It's not easy being surrounded by a bunch of ill-informed malcontents and backstabbing so-called *friends*. The temptations to take advantage of certain *perks* can be subtle and insidious, as Spicer has demonstrated. If you're not interested in running for office, seems like all you have to do is tell Sarah that and you can get on with the rest of your lives together."

"I wish it were that easy, Gramps, but she's got it into her head that staying married to her will only drag down my architecture career and stymie any other opportunities that might come my way. She points out that it didn't take the senator and his wife very long to discover the skeleton in her closet. She figures it's just a matter of time before other people do the same."

"If they do," Edgar said, "you acknowledge it and keep trucking. People who know you won't run away screaming. You'd be surprised how forgiving people can be when you tell them the truth."

"I agree, but she doesn't see it that way. She keeps pointing out that Clyburn Estates depends on people being able to trust us to give them an honest deal. We need a good reputation, not only with clients but with lending institutions. An open line of low-interest credit is our lifeblood. She's afraid once word gets out that she was a…call girl, our corporate name will be permanently tarnished, if not completely ruined. The public won't want to do business with us, and banks will refuse to grant us the short-term loans we depend on."

Edgar chuckled. "I think she has an idealized view of the corporate world and its affinity for virtue, but putting that aside, why would her past get out if you're not running for office?"

"Because it's a matter of public record. Jane Spicer told her anything I do that requires public or private confidence is in jeopardy because of her immoral past."

"Political scare tactics, son. It's not as if Sarah were Heidi Fleiss or—" he almost said another name "—Sydney Biddle Barrows."

"Who?"

"The Mayflower Madam. Besides, Sarah doesn't even work for us." Edgar looked over. "Does she?"

"No, and we have no plans for her to. Actually, I was hoping she'd be pregnant by now."

"I did talk to you about the birds and the bees, didn't I?"

Bram finally laughed. "Yes, Gramps. So did Dad and Uncle Kyle and Uncle Walter."

Edgar snickered. "There's nothing like a good education."

"Sarah wants to be a stay-at-home mom, and that's what I want, too," Bram went on a minute later. "But now she's not even sure she should have kids. Says it would be unfair for them to have a former prostitute for a mother. In her mind, there are some scars, like sex crimes and murder, that never go away."

Edgar pinched his lower lip between thumb and forefinger. "She could be right, I suppose."

Bram shot him a round-eyed glare, displeased with the observation. He'd expected—wanted—his grandfather to reject the notion out of hand.

He turned off the loop onto Highway 87, which led them past Goodfellow Air Force Base, became South Chadbourne Street and carried them into the heart of San Angelo. Immediately across the bridge over the Concho River he turned right onto Concho Avenue, the oldest street in the city. Lovingly restored late-nineteenth- and early-twentieth-century brick-and-stone buildings lined the north side. An old-fashioned wooden sidewalk ran in front of them.

"I just can't seem to convince her that divorce isn't the solution," Bram muttered. "She made a mistake. A big mistake. But she can't let it ruin the rest of her life, our lives. I've reminded her I asked her to marry me with my eyes wide open, but she says it doesn't matter."

He started checking the diagonal parking spaces in front of Eggemeyer's General Store, the place that sold the confections they'd been dispatched to buy, but it was Saturday afternoon, the emporium was packed with tourists, and all the parking slots were filled.

Edgar had grown thoughtful as he surveyed the busy avenue. He glanced at a sign hanging above a jewelry store on the opposite side of the street, and a smile slowly spread across his face. Of course. That was why Evvie has sent them here on this wild-goose chase.

"Maybe your grandmother will be able to help."

"I sure hope so. I can't imagine what she could tell Sarah that I haven't."

Edgar threw back his head and laughed. "My boy, you'd be surprised."

Bram gave him a quizzical expression.

"Did I ever tell you how I met your grandmother?" Edgar asked.

"All I know is that you got married right after the Second World War," Bram replied as he waited behind another car for the light to change.

"We have plenty of time before we have to go back. Let's grab a cup of joe in the café on the corner," Edgar suggested, "and I'll tell you all about it."

As baffled as ever about what his grandparents were up to, Bram obediently swung the pickup around and found a spot in a vacant lot a few doors down from Miss Hattie's Bordello Museum.

Chapter 3

The two women returned to the patio, Sarah carrying the tray Evvie had set with a large floral-patterned teapot, matching cups and saucers, sugar and lemon, silver spoons and small lace-trimmed napkins. Evvie brought an opened bottle of Cherry Herring and two small crystal aperitif glasses. While the younger woman poured their tea, her husband's grandmother served the ruby-red liqueur.

"I'm glad it's not windy today," Evvie commented. "It's so much nicer to be able to sit out here."

She poured their tea and added lemon to her own.

"Let me tell you a story, my dear."

She took a sip of her tea and settled back in her wicker peacock chair. "On February 2 of 1941, I turned sixteen. Groundhog Day. My brother, Henry, used to tease me about it, saying I was the one who always scared the little critter back into his hole. In response, I would preen and remind him that that meant I was responsible for spring being just around the corner.

"Not that Henry could brag. He was born on April Fools' Day, which made him the butt of a lot of jokes, too, most of which he told on himself. He liked to laugh, did Henry, and he was always able to make the people around him laugh. He was two years older than me and I positively adored him.

"My mother said she never had to worry about where I was because I'd be with my big brother. The problem was that Henry was the adventurous type, so she could never predict where he might have led me off to. Oh, he got annoyed with me once in a while for trailing after him like a shadow, especially when he wanted to play roughhouse with his pals, but he tolerated me well enough. That isn't to say he didn't pick on me some-times, but heaven help anyone else who tried it. Henry was my champion, my fearless protector.

"Two years before that—in '39—Dad's younger brother, John, lost his wife to flu, right after she'd given birth to their second child, a girl. Uncle John earned adequate enough wages driving a tractor on one of the big ranches, but with Aunt Louise gone there wasn't much money left over after he paid a woman to mind the kids all day while he was out in the fields. So when we lost our farm in Oklahoma to the drought, he suggested we come to Texas and share his rented house in town. With his steady income, Dad and Henry grabbing whatever jobs they could find, and Mom keeping house and taking care of the kids, there'd be enough money for us to get by on.

"My folks really didn't have any choice. Our house and land were gone, and there wasn't even day work available in our part of Oklahoma. So in December of '40 we packed up and headed south to San Angelo.

"Things didn't get better, though.

"Dad's health had always been edgy. He'd been gassed in the First World War and never completely recovered. Even though he'd never smoked, he had what they used to call a smoker's cough. I reckon all the dust he inhaled working in the fields from sunup to sundown didn't help any.

"As soon as we arrived in San Angelo, Uncle John became concerned about Dad's constant hacking and coughing, and when he saw Dad spitting up blood, he sent him to the public health clinic. The doctor there fluoroscoped him and said he might have TB. You don't hear much about tuberculosis nowadays, but there was a lot of it back then, before they developed all these wonder drugs. The doc sent Dad up to the McKnight Sanitarium in Carlsbad, twenty miles northwest of town, where he could be x-rayed and have other tests run. Turned out he had a galloping case of TB, and he was contagious, too, so they quarantined him there and wouldn't even let him come home.

"My brother nabbed whatever work he could find,

but there wasn't much available, nothing steady or that paid real well. Henry hated being idle, feeling useless, so in January of '41 he hopped the rails and rode a boxcar out to California to join thousands of other down-and-out Okies. He picked fruit in citrus groves, vegetables on truck farms, worked on road gangs, you name it, and he sent money home when he could, but the work wasn't dependable and he had to live, too, so the money was never very much or all that regular. He kept promising to send more, but we knew it wasn't easy for him, either. He was eighteen, healthy and a good worker, but all the steady jobs went to older men with families.

"So Henry wasn't home that Groundhog Day when I turned sweet sixteen, and I missed him dreadfully. He did send me a postcard from California, though, to wish me a happy birthday. I still have it. A penny postcard was cheaper than three cents for a first-class stamp on an envelope and the ten-cent price of a card. Naturally I was thrilled to receive it. Fresno, California, the postmark said. The place sounded so romantic to me. I wished with all my heart I could still trail after my big brother.

"Three days later the tractor Uncle John was driving flipped over and killed him. He had been our sole source of income, and suddenly he was gone. Now we were even worse off than we'd been back in Oklahoma. My father was languishing in the sanitarium in Carlsbad. My brother was far from home in California, and Mom now had the added burden of raising Uncle John's two orphaned children.

"I dropped out of high school to find work, but there just wasn't any. Mom applied for government assistance, and our local church was able to help a little. Still, we had barely enough to pay the twenty-dollars-a-month rent, the utilities and put food on the table.

"Mama took in washing and ironing when she could, but so did half the women in town. It was back-breaking work, bending over a scrub board, hanging wet wash, dipping collars and cuffs in scalding starch, ironing everything with flatirons we heated on the gas stove. I helped when I could, but the thing I was really good at was sewing.

"Every day I'd walk from house to house in the Santa Rita area of San Angelo on the west side of the Concho, where the better-off people lived, asking housewives and sometimes maids if they had any darning or sewing I could do for them. Nobody darns socks anymore, but people did in those days. Nothing went to waste. The piecework paid only pennies, but a nickel would buy a pound of flour or a pound of potatoes. A quart of milk cost a dime. So did a dozen eggs.

"That year we ate a lot of vanilla pudding. Mama made it from scratch. Oh, it was so good. She devised all kinds of ways of fixing potatoes, too. One of my favorites was when she quartered them with the skins still on, put them in a pan, poured diluted ketchup over them and baked them in the oven. We ate everything, even the crispy skins. I still get funny looks from people in restaurants when I put ketchup on my baked potato, but what's wrong with that? They put it on their French fries. Some of my friends grew to hate potatoes. Thought of them as poverty food. I, on the other hand, don't much care for beans. We ate an awful lot of them, as well.

"For me the best day of the week was Wednesday, when Mama received whatever money Henry was able to send. If there was enough, we'd feast on bacon and eggs, grits and buttered white toast rather than the biscuits Mom made using wood ash instead of baking powder. On Wednesday nights we went to bed with full tummies and smiles on our faces.

"One hot July afternoon I was sitting in the shade on the front porch of Mrs. Sedlak's house in Santa Rita, adjusting the waist on one of her silk dresses, when a black-and-maroon LaSalle roadster pulled up at the curb. At first I fancied the woman who got out must be a movie star. She had shiny auburn hair piled high on her head, a feathery hat, and she was very smartly dressed. She even had on the proper white gloves ladies wore in those days when they went calling. As she drew closer, I could see her makeup was pretty heavy, and she was older than I first thought, probably in her sixties, but she carried herself with the deportment of a queen.

"She greeted me pleasantly and introduced herself as Miss Hattie. Her glittering jewelry jangled and I got a whiff of expensive perfume when she leaned over to examine what I was doing. I felt intimidated by this rich woman, but I was also thrilled when she complimented me on my fine stitches. Maybe, I thought, maybe she'll hire me to sew for her, too.

"An hour later, as she was leaving the house, she and Mrs. Sedlak stopped and gazed at me strangely for a long minute. My heart began to race. Had I done something wrong? My hands began to sweat, not good when you're handling silk. Then Miss Hattie asked me if I would like to sew for her part-time at her place of business.

"I was ecstatic. She said she would pay me five dollars a week to start with, and if I had to be there more than twenty hours, she'd pay me twenty-five cents for every additional hour. Five dollars sounds pitiful now, but it didn't then. It meant we might be able to have bacon and eggs more than once a week.

"She gave me her address. Eighteen and a half East Concho Avenue. Right in the heart of downtown San Angelo. But she told me not to enter that way. Instead I should go through the dry-goods store at number eighteen and out the back door, then climb the wooden stairs to the second floor. The servants' entrance, I figured.

"I thanked her profusely. She smiled at her friend, returned to her fancy car and drove away.

"Mrs. Sedlak gave me a quizzical expression. 'Do you know who she is?'

"'Miss Hattie,' I replied, feeling more lighthearted than I had in ages. *Wait till I tell Mama.* I'd never brought home more than three dollars in one week, though sometimes people paid me in food. Once I got a big apple pie for an afternoon of darning. It was our supper that night. Oh, how we feasted.

"'I used to work for Miss Hattie some years ago. Do you know what kind of business she runs?'

"I had been so excited about the prospect of a regular cash-paying job, even if it was only part-time, that I hadn't even thought to ask. A boardinghouse maybe or a small factory where they made things. Why she would require a steady seamstress for businesses like those had never crossed my mind.

"'Miss Hattie runs the finest gentlemen's club in San Angelo,' the woman said, a thinly drawn eyebrow raised as she waited for my reaction.

"'A gentlemen's club?' I didn't understand what that meant.

"Mrs. Sedlak closed her eyes and shook her head. 'A bordello.'

Sarah's eyes went wide. "She was a madam?"

Evvie filled the two small aperitif glasses with the sweet cherry liqueur and passed one to her guest.

"Miss Hattie wasn't *a* madam, my dear. She was *the* madam. Her place was famous. I didn't realize that at the time, of course. I was still reeling from the fact that the kindly woman I'd been sewing for had just announced she was a retired prostitute, and the lady who'd offered me a stable job ran a brothel."

Evvie chuckled. "I was completely shocked. I'd never met a fallen woman before—not that I was aware of, anyway—and I'm sure my mouth fell open as I stared at Mrs. Sedlak. I'd grown up on a farm, so I understood about sex, but I hadn't experienced it. I'd let a boy kiss me once, but that was as far as we'd gone.

From church I'd learned sex before marriage was a terrible sin, and prostitution...well, that was even worse, an abomination in the eyes of the Lord—and the community.

"I was so disappointed. I needed work desperately and this woman had offered me more money than I'd ever earned. But I couldn't take the job. I just couldn't. What would my mother say? And my father? What would Henry say if he got wind of it?

"Still, my mind commenced to stray into places it shouldn't. In spite of going hungry on occasion, I was healthy enough, and while I tried not to dwell on it, sex was fascinating. What was it like? I wondered.

"I knew boys enjoyed it, but what about girls? The reports I'd received from the few I'd met who'd actually tried it were mixed. They all agreed it was painful the first time, but some of them said it was fun after that— at least with the right boy.

"Well, I wasn't going to find out, not until I got married. The very idea of having sex with strangers... It was disgusting, demeaning, shameful, completely out of the question, so ridiculous and immoral that I couldn't even mention Miss Hattie's offer to my mother.

"Work in a house of prostitution? Never.

"Yet all night long, as my stomach grumbled and I reflected on the kids asking for more food, and my mother giving them her supper after putting in a long day's work over a washtub, I began to rationalize.

"Okay, so it was a house of ill repute—already my mind was using more genteel euphemisms to describe it—but I wasn't being expected to do anything sinful there. Just sew clothes. There was nothing wrong with sewing clothes. Everybody had a right to wear properly fitted garments, even…soiled doves. Sewing was how I could help the family, the people who depended on me.

"The next morning I made the rounds of the newer homes in Santa Rita. At one house I fixed the hem of a dress and darned a few socks and got a plate of biscuits and pan gravy for my efforts. I hadn't eaten breakfast, so the food was welcome and filling, but it wasn't helping anyone at home. If I'd been able to earn some money, any money, that morning, maybe I wouldn't have made the decision I finally made.

"I kept thinking about the two hungry young kids at home and Dad being a charity case in the TB sanitarium. He would undoubtedly be up there for a while, yet as soon as he ceased to be contagious they'd send him home. He probably wouldn't be able to work, but he'd be another mouth to feed. My mother was already wearing herself out washing clothes and taking care of the children. If anything happened to her, what would become of us?

"Around noon I headed downtown. I paced anxiously along the south side of Concho Avenue. Number eighteen was across the street. A dry-goods store, just like Miss Hattie had said. Ladies were casually strolling in and coming out with bundles neatly wrapped in brown paper and twine. To the right was an inconspicuous doorway. Above it, written in gold leaf, were the numbers *eighteen and a half.*

"Screwing up my courage, I darted between honking

Model A's and chain-driven trucks, stepped over horse droppings and managed to safely cross the busy thoroughfare. There, catching my breath, I entered the store.

"Several women were fingering bolts of fabric, examining buttons and buckles, talking to clerks. I'd planned to walk through the place and go directly out the back door, but it wasn't that easy.

"I hadn't had a new dress in two years, and even that hadn't really been new, just a hand-me-down from one of my cousins in Oklahoma. Since then I'd been altering a few of my mother's old dresses to fit me, which meant she had even fewer things to wear.

"Now I was confronted with a veritable wonderland of fabrics. Cotton and linen, wool, even the new rayon. Such bright colors. Floral and geometric patterns, tweeds, plaids, stripes, polka dots. Everything a young girl could ask for.

"I kept my distance from the silks and satins, content to admire them from afar, since there was no way I could even dream of buying remnants to use as accent pieces, but on one of the side rows they had printed cotton broadcloth, ginghams and calicos. It was impossible for me to resist the temptation to run my hands over the bolts, to feel the clean new material between my fingers. One of the salesclerks kept eyeing me. Maybe he thought I was going to steal something, but he didn't say anything and he didn't approach me.

"After a couple of minutes, I slipped out the back. To my left were the wooden stairs Miss Hattie had told me about leading up to the second floor.

"My legs felt like jelly as I mounted the steps. At the top I found a single door. Through the glass panel I could make out a long shadowy corridor with doors on both sides. Biting my lips, my heart in my mouth, I reached for the knob."

Chapter 4

Bram pulled the truck into the parking lot between the nineteenth-century two-story buildings on the north side of Concho Avenue and switched off the grumbling diesel engine. They walked back to the sidewalk. Edgar looked across the street to the furniture store that had originally been a carriage house. There'd been a couple of bars years ago—private clubs, since the town was dry back them.

They bore left.

Edgar remembered when the coffee shop they entered on the corner had been the office of a small gas station. The twin pumps were long gone. Containered decorative trees and colorful planters now blocked what had once been the driveway.

So much had changed, yet the external forms were still there.

They took a table by the window. A waitress came up and greeted them, pad and pencil in hand.

"What can I get you gents?" she asked.

Both men ordered coffee.

"Think you can put up with an old man reminiscing?" Edgar asked.

Bram smiled. "Try me."

The old man gazed into space a minute before starting.

"In October of '40 I turned nineteen. My parents were evangelical missionaries, and we were living in South China at the time. We'd fled from the northeast when the Japanese invaded in '37, but they were so hell-bent on further conquest that my father was finally persuaded we had to get out of the country for my mother's safety and mine. So, in March of '41 we boarded a steamer for the United States.

"We stopped off in San Angelo on our journey from California to the East Coast to visit a cousin of my father's and to preach in the local community in the hope of raising funds for his new mission assignment. In spite of the depression that was still gripping the country, people were incredibly generous with their meager cash.

"My parents were being transferred to a church school in the Belgian Congo, and they wanted me to go with them, but I balked. As much as I respected what they were doing, their calling wasn't mine.

"Missionaries always seem to minister to the poor rather than the rich, so I'd seen my share of poverty. Hunger is the same no matter where you are. I wanted to experience more of life. The newspapers and books I'd read, and especially the glossy magazines like *Look* and *Life* made me aware of a vastly different world. I'd been born in the States, but I'd lived most of my life overseas, so for me America was the great adventure. I decided it was time for me to sample it firsthand, and what better place to start than Texas.

"Ezekiel, my father's cousin, owned an automobile dealership here in town. When I announced my intention to stay behind, he offered me a job selling cars for him. I pointed out that I didn't have any experience as a commercial salesman, and he reminded me I'd been helping my father sell the Word of God all my life. I don't think my parents ever picked up on the cynicism in Zeke's comparison. He said I had both the looks and the personality to excel in his trade. Very flattering, but almost from the moment I met Cousin Zeke I'd glommed on to the fact that he was a pip who could have sold snake oil as well as used cars, and I marveled at my folks' naiveté in never recognizing it themselves. That was all right. I figured if dear Cousin Zeke could use me, there was no reason I couldn't return the favor.

"My parents said goodbye, happy in the knowledge that I was staying with family, had a good job and was in a community that respected the ways of the Lord.

"Little did they know.

"With Zeke's expert coaching, I managed to sell a couple of flivvers to unsuspecting marks. I have to admit I enjoyed the challenge, at least with my first sale. I figured the crotchety old cheapskate who bought it deserved what he got, but a modicum of my parents' moral righteousness must have rubbed off, because my second sale to a hardscrabble family produced nothing but painful nightmares. I kept picturing them breaking down on a desolate road and dying of hunger and thirst, or being devoured by a pack of coyotes. So I sought them out, warned them about the automobile's flaws and returned my commission to help them defray repair costs. Their gratitude was so profuse they made me feel even worse about selling them the piece of crap in the first place.

"Not wanting to go through that kind of experience again—and knowing I couldn't financially afford to— I talked to Cousin Zeke about letting me sell new cars, which were presumably more reliable.

"Zeke wasn't overly enthusiastic about the idea. His bread and butter was in the large number of jalopies he sold. He bought them for next to nothing, sometimes from junkyards, and resold them at obscenely inflated prices. He preferred to deal with his well-heeled customers personally, especially since the commission on new cars was considerably higher because they were more expensive, and he didn't have to share it with anyone.

"He finally relented, though, when I offered to take

only a half commission on my first sale. Waving money in front of Zeke worked every time."

"So how did you do selling *new* cars?" Bram asked.

Edgar chuckled. "Selling new cars seemed like a brilliant idea when I struck my bargain with Cousin Zeke. What I'd blithely failed to recognize was that there wasn't much of a local market for them. This, of course, was why Zeke dealt mostly in jalopies. Back in '41 ordinary people were still struggling to make ends meet. There wasn't much money left over for luxury automobiles, certainly not new ones."

Their coffee arrived in thick crockery mugs.

"Plus—" Edgar wrapped his long bony fingers around the steaming brew "—farmers and ranchers were notoriously land rich and cash poor. Not to mention having an annoying talent for keeping their old tin cans running on bubble gum and baling wire. A new family sedan was definitely not high on anybody's list of priorities."

"Cousin Zeke must have thought he could sell them to somebody," Bram observed.

His grandfather nodded. "The only people who might have the dough and who cared enough about their images to spend it on automobiles were doctors, lawyers, wealthy widows and crooks. Zeke had already approached most of the sawbones and mouthpieces in town who might be interested."

"What about oilmen?"

They could certainly afford luxury and styling, but they bought those kinds of cars only for their families.

Personal transportation was based on utility rather than comfort. Besides, most of them lived in Midland."

"So I guess that left wealthy widows and crooks," Bram said wryly.

"Yeah, well, well-heeled dowagers were notoriously tightfisted with their moola."

"Which brings us to the criminal class."

The old man smirked. "After I beat my head against a few stone walls, Zeke took pity on me and steered me toward the one person he thought might be in the market for a brand-new Packard convertible coupe—which he described as the bee's knees in styling."

"Who was that?"

"The town's foremost madam, Miss Hattie."

"You mean there really was a Miss Hattie?"

Edgar laughed. "Yes, my boy, there really was a Miss Hattie."

"So you got to the top of the stairs," Sarah said almost breathlessly, "and reached for the doorknob, and…"

Evvie enjoyed a sip of her Cherry Herring. "A tiny bell over the door jingled when I opened it. I stuck my head in and saw a scrawny black man in baggy pants and a frayed white shirt rise from a wooden chair a few feet away. My first impulse was to turn around and bolt, but before I had a chance, Miss Hattie stuck her head out of a room down the hall and started toward us.

"'That's all right, Elmo,' she said. 'I'll take care of this.'

"'Yessum,' he responded with a respectful nod and resumed his seat.

"She smiled kindly at me. 'I'm glad you came, Evvie.'

"I should have said something in reply, but I didn't know what. In truth I'm not sure my voice would have worked at that moment.

"She patted my hands, which I had bunched at my waist, as if to indicate she understood my shyness, and asked me to follow her to the dining room, which turned out to be at the opposite end of the long narrow building."

Evvie savored another sip of her liqueur.

"I knew I should keep my eyes directly ahead of me as I walked behind her down the dim hall, but of course I couldn't. This was forbidden territory and naturally it fascinated me. On both sides of the corridor were small rooms. Each had a screen door that opened out. For air circulation, of course. This was long before air-conditioning, but it also let me—and any customers walking through—see into the rooms.

"A young woman with the most beautiful long blond hair was sprawled on a bed on her stomach, reading a magazine, her cleavage on display. She peered up as I passed by and smiled at me. I panicked. Should I smile back? Would she think I was one of *them?* I walked on quickly.

"The next room on the right had a shade pulled down on the inside of the screen door. I could hear bedsprings squeaking and a man grunting. I'm sure my face flared beet red.

"I rushed on and this time I was even more surprised to hear a baby cry for a few seconds. When we reached that room, I saw a young woman sitting in a chair between her bed and a cradle, breast-feeding an infant."

"My God!" Sarah exclaimed. "A new mother and she was back to turning tricks? That's incredible."

Evvie smiled. "I got to meet her later. She was a wonderful mom. Took real good care of her little boy."

Sarah shook her head, trying to process everything. "So what happened next?"

"Miss Hattie led me through a parlor with settees and fiddleback chairs to one of the two rooms over-looking the street. This one had a big pedestal table. Around the corner was a tiny little kitchen."

"Oh, did they serve food there, like at a tavern or a nightclub?"

Evvie shook her head. "Miss Hattie occasionally put out little snacks in the evening, but nothing that required cooking. All the girls' meals were ordered in from a restaurant a few doors down. The kitchen wasn't much, a three-burner gas stove, an icebox and a sink. They could keep things warm in the oven if they had to, or heat up a can of soup. The main thing it was used for was making coffee and tea.

"She sat me down at the round table and explained what she wanted me to do. Mostly mend dresses and undergarments and alter clothes the girls had bought or were trading with one another. If I did well, she said, she might ask me to make clothes on the treadle sewing machine she had in the card room. Not when the room was in use, of course. She promised to pay me extra for that work. I was to work weekdays from eight until around noon. Most of the girls didn't get up until after ten, and they normally didn't have their first callers until lunchtime. If any men did show up while I was there, she said I should just ignore them."

Sarah smiled with amusement.

"I was to be polite, of course," Evvie continued, "but only speak when spoken to and not linger. That was fine with me. I planned on staying completely out of their way."

"How long did you stay there?"

"I sewed at Miss Hattie's for about a month."

"A month? That's all?"

Evvie smiled.

Chapter 5

"I always used to think of hookers as coming from the lowest rungs of society," Sarah said, "uneducated, desperate women who have no alternative but to sell themselves. Then I got involved with the sorority and found out it wasn't necessarily like that.

"We called ourselves escorts, companions, even geishas—never prostitutes, but of course that's what we were. Women selling sex. Some of the girls were from prominent families and very well-off, so it wasn't all about the money. None of us was poor, and we certainly weren't illiterate."

"So why did you do it?" Evvie asked.

Sarah shrugged at the same time she avoided the other woman's eyes. "The excitement, I guess. The excitement of getting away with doing something forbidden, I guess. And for me the money was a factor. I wasn't going to starve without it, but it sure helped make life easier, more fun."

Clearly embarrassed by the admission, Sarah kept her face averted.

"It was a little different for the girls at Miss Hattie's," Evvie said. She gazed out over the parched landscape, listened to the distant moo of a cow.

"Let's see. There was Miss Blue. Her real name was Dorothea Kraus. She was twenty years old, had lustrous brown hair and baby-blue eyes. A bit chubby, but her skin was beautifully smooth and flawless. Pink and white. Sort of pixieish. She always wore blue. Blue dresses, blue blouses, blue hats, blue gloves. Her room was painted blue. Even the sheets on her bed were dyed blue. She was the youngest of twelve children. Her mother had died of breast cancer when she was eight. At fourteen she was raped by one of her cousins. Her father blamed her, said she shouldn't have led him on. He called her a tramp and refused to talk to her after that. A year later, she ran away from home. She'd been at Miss Hattie's about three years when I first met her."

"That's terrible," Sarah said, "and so unfair."

Evvie tilted her head to one side. "It was a common attitude back then. There were no support groups in those days. If a woman got raped or molested it was somehow her fault. Rape victims were often blamed for what was done to them and became social outcasts. They were the real soiled doves."

Sarah shook her head.

"I've already told you about Miss Mable. She was the one with the baby. Her real name was Mable Higginbottom. Twenty-three, brunette, with lovely soft brown eyes."

Evvie paused. "Who else? Miss Kitty. Her name was Eula Mae Fargus. Pretty little thing, barely five feet tall, with porcelain skin, pitch-black hair and dark blue eyes. She was eighteen when we first met. Her parents had been killed in a train wreck when she was ten, and she was put in an orphanage. Not a very nice one, either, if there ever was such a thing. The matron beat the girls for even the smallest infractions of her rules and held back food to save money. Kitty was malnourished when she finally ran away at thirteen. Lost her virginity a year later as the price for food and shelter. She'd been at Miss Hattie's about two years when I got there."

"They were all so young."

"Miss Hattie's patrons preferred young girls for several reasons. They tended to be better looking and were less apt to carry disease. There was also the illusion of innocence, which appealed to a certain element of her clientele."

"Sounds like rape to me. Sick."

Evvie nodded. "Some women have rape fantasies, too, my dear, so it's not completely fair to condemn only men for them. As long as they don't act on them, of course."

Her mouth twisted in disgust, Sarah only grunted.

"I already mentioned Miss Goldie," Evvie continued.

"Her real name was Clarissa Porch. She was twenty-two but acted a lot older. She had the most luxurious blond hair. Real, too, not out of a bottle. Washed it with two eggs and a bottle of beer twice a week so that it shone like spun gold. She was, as the saying goes, stacked. Really slim waist and, well, let's just say Dolly Parton had nothing on Goldie. She was the only one of the girls who had actually chosen to be a hooker. Seems her father caught her in the act with her boyfriend in the hayloft when she was seventeen, called down the wrath of God and threw her out of the house. The way she told it, she figured if she was going to hell, she might as well enjoy the trip, and didn't see any reason she shouldn't be paid for the entertainment she provided along the way. She moved to San Angelo, freelanced for a while, then went to work for Miss Hattie."

"I get the impression she wasn't a very nice person," Sarah commented.

Evvie chuckled. "She could be pleasant enough, even charming when she wanted to be, but she was also shrewd and selfish. As a result, she didn't have any close friends among the other girls, but frankly I doubt she cared. She liked men. Of all the girls there, I think she was the only one who thoroughly enjoyed what she did."

Evvie took another sip of her liqueur. "Finally there was Miss Rosie, Rosamund Kearner. Auburn hair, hazel eyes and a lovely smile. Rosie always wore red of one shade or another, ranging anywhere from pale rose to dazzling scarlet. She was the best educated of the girls, actually had a high-school diploma, which she proudly displayed on her wall. She was twenty-four. As I said, the oldest of Miss Hattie's girls and the most mature. Everybody seemed to gravitate to her with their secrets and to ask her advice. She was also the only one who had a two-room suite."

Evvie fingered the base of her liqueur glass as she went on.

"They kept me real busy those first few weeks, mainly because they hadn't had a regular seamstress in over a year. The last one, according to Miss Kitty, was an old black woman who dropped dead of a massive stroke while sewing a piece of lace to the bodice on one of her dresses. Miss Hattie hadn't been able to find anyone she felt she could trust since then.

"You have to remember many of her clients were prominent members of the community. Most were also married, so of course they didn't want it bantered about that they visited a bawdy house. As you might expect, the back door was used much more than the one on Concho Avenue. Gentlemen would go into the bank next door, slip out the rear and use the steps I'd come up by.

"During the first week I did pretty ordinary things. Mostly mending torn hems and split seams and replacing missing buttons. I was amazed that some of the girls didn't have a clue about sewing, could barely thread a needle, but once they realized how good I was they started presenting me with all sorts of requests, like removing out-of-style accessories to streamline dresses or adding trim to accent lines.

"That meant I occasionally stayed later than noon,

which I didn't mind because it earned me extra money, but it also meant gentlemen callers caught glimpses of me in the card room or the parlor. I didn't reckon there was much chance of them talking about me being in a bordello or of word getting back to my mother, but a few of them started giving me the once-over. I can't deny feeling a bit flattered. At the same time I was embarrassed that they thought of me *that way*.

"I earned five dollars my first full week and seven the second. I gave all of it to my mother. As you can imagine she was thrilled to receive it, but she also wanted to know where it came from.

"I didn't want to lie to her, but I also had no doubt that, as much as we needed the money, she'd be furious if she realized the type of establishment I was spending my time in, and she'd absolutely forbid me to go back. So I told her I'd met a wealthy society lady who was very generous. She hadn't had anyone to sew for her in a long time and needed me to alter a bunch of dresses. It wasn't a lie exactly. Miss Hattie did have a lot of money, and she was generous, and the girls who worked for her did have clothes that required fixing. Mama would have objected to me calling her a lady, but that was just quibbling, I told myself.

"In my second week I got talking with Miss Mable, the one with the baby. It turned out her husband, Arthur—"

"She was married?" Sarah exclaimed. "Oh, you mean divorced."

Evvie smiled and shook her head. "Arthur had been

stricken with infectious tuberculosis and was quarantined at the McKnight Sanitarium, like my dad. Having no family, no place to go, no money, unable to find a job on her own and desperate, Mable finally went to Miss Hattie."

"Surely she didn't tell her husband what she was doing."

"She didn't have much choice after she got pregnant."

Almost as if she was afraid of the answer, Sarah asked, "What was his reaction?"

"He wasn't thrilled, but he agreed they should keep the baby."

Sarah's eyebrows shot up. "I don't imagine many guys would be that generous or understanding."

Evvie smiled. "I told her how much I missed my dad, that we hadn't seen him in three months because we'd had to sell Uncle John's truck to pay his funeral expenses and didn't have any way to get up there.

"She told me one of her regulars would probably be willing to drive me, Mom and the kids for a couple of dollars, enough to pay for gas with maybe a little left over for his time. His name was Slim, and he called on Mable every Thursday. She offered to talk to him about it and introduce us.

"The idea of actually meeting one of the customers unnerved me. I mean, how was I supposed to look him in the eye and not think about why he was there? But if he could help us get to visit Dad...

"'There is one thing,' I told Mable, 'I don't want him to say anything to my mom—'

"'About where you work. Don't worry, Evvie. I don't think he's inclined to announce, especially to a woman, that he patronizes a whorehouse.'

"I purposely saved up some of the extra sewing the other girls wanted me to do until Thursday so I could stay a little later than usual and be there when Slim arrived.

"He and Mable went to her room and drew the shade for privacy. A half hour later they came to the card room, where I was busy at the treadle sewing machine.

"Mable introduced us and explained to him what I wanted.

"Based on the guy's name I'd pictured a rangy, handsome cowboy in his twenties. Well, he was rangy, all right but not at all handsome, and instead of being a cowboy, he was a Fuller Brush man in his late thirties. He didn't sound Texan, either. Spoke with a strange accent I later learned was Welsh. Its soft lilt fascinated me.

"I could feel his eyes examining me. 'When would you like to go?'

"'Sunday after church,' I said, 'if that's okay.'

"He asked for my address. I gave it to him and offered to pay him in advance, which Mable later told me was a foolish thing to do. With the money already in his pocket he had no reason to show up, and what could I do? Who would I complain to?

"He refused to take it, however, and said I could pay him when we got back.

"On my way home I realized I'd left an awful lot to

chance. We hadn't worked out a cover story for my mom, for example, about where I'd met him.

"Mom was ecstatic when I told her we'd be going up to Carlsbad on Sunday.

"Slim showed up at one o'clock, as he'd promised. He was very polite to my mother, even helped her into the backseat of his battered old Model A. The kids sat beside her and I sat in front with him.

"'How did you and Evvie meet?' Mom asked Slim after we were under way. 'She never did tell me.'

"He glanced over at me and I realized he was amused.

"'I sell brushes and things door-to-door, ma'am. Evvie was sewing for a woman when I stopped by to see her.'

"Giving me a wink, he questioned my mother about where in Oklahoma we hailed from and what we did there.

"Mom told him all about the farm we used to have, and I realized as she prattled on how lonely she must have been for adult company. In no time we arrived at Dr. McKnight's sanitarium.

"Dad was sitting under a canvas umbrella in an Adirondack chair on a lawn with a lot of other people, mostly men. We'd been told by the nurse who brought us to him that we shouldn't kiss or make physical contact, since he was still contagious, but Mom couldn't help herself. All teary, she threw her arms around him. He accepted the embrace for a minute. I spied the loneliness in his eyes as he eased her away. He was even thinner than I remembered. His skin seemed loose, almost translucent, and he appeared decades older than his forty-two years. I couldn't obey the rules, either. I threw my arms around him and cried.

"I refused to acknowledge it, even to myself, but I think I knew at that moment he was dying. I loved my dad. He was someone I could always count on. He smiled at me, commented on how good I looked, how grown-up, and told me I was even prettier than he remembered.

"'I better get home soon and oil the shotgun,' he said with a big grin. I'm sure I blushed.

"He was such a good man, never hurt a soul, but the world was treating him so unfairly. He'd lost both his parents in a tornado back in '34. Lost the farm he and Mom had slaved over all the years of their married life. His younger brother had been killed in a stupid accident, and now our family was splintered. Henry out in California. Dad stuck here, a charity case. It didn't seem fair that a good and faithful servant should be treated this cruelly, and it made me mad.

"'They say I might be able to leave here soon,' he told us.

"I hoped so, but I worried his release would bring new problems, another mouth to feed for one. At the sanitarium it was clear Dad was an invalid, a sick person who needed to be taken care of. At home he'd feel compelled to find a job, but looking at him I realized no one would hire him, not for very long anyway. He was too weak to put in a full day's work. He'd feel like a failure, and I couldn't bear to see that happen.

"I had to find out what it would cost to keep him

there until he was well enough to be productive, if only for his pride's sake. So while he and Mom talked, I wandered off to the administration building for answers.

"They did things a lot different in those days. Across the road from the McKnight Sanitarium was a tent city where the families of many of the patients lived. Dr. McKnight provided the medical treatment, free of charge if they couldn't afford it, but he expected the relatives of patients to feed and clothe their kin and attend to their daily needs. In cases such as ours, where family members couldn't hang around, the sanitarium picked up the tab, but for obvious reasons they discharged those patients as quickly as possible.

"The administrator I spoke to thanked me for stopping by and said she would have sought me out if I hadn't. Since we weren't feeding my father or doing his laundry, she wanted to know if it would be possible for us to make at least a small monetary contribution to his maintenance. She said it cost them about five dollars a day to keep a patient. She realized we couldn't afford that much, but if we could contribute one dollar a day, that would at least pay for his food.

"A dollar a day. Thirty dollars a month. We were barely getting by on fifty dollars or less. A dollar a day was about what I was earning as a seamstress. Five days a week, not seven. It put more and better food on the table, but if I sent that money to the sanitarium, we'd be back to vanilla pudding, beans and rice and bacon and eggs only once a week.

"I promised to send what I could. The woman

smiled and thanked me, but I could tell she didn't believe I'd be sending anything.

"Mom was on a seesaw during the ride back to San Angelo. One minute she would claim Dad looked so much better, which wasn't true, that he was eager to come home, which he was, and how much she wanted him there. I certainly believed that part. They'd been married twenty years and shared everything together. When I thought about marriage, I envisioned what they had. I'd seen her cry on Dad's shoulder when they had to pack up and leave the farm in Oklahoma, how glassy his eyes were as he hugged her and tried to assure her things would improve, that one day they'd get it all back. I'm sure they both knew it wasn't likely to happen, but they found strength and comfort in each other. Now Mom was all alone. She spent her days scrubbing other people's clothes, washing dirty diapers, fixing meals that were barely adequate and that sometimes she didn't even get to eat.

"Halfway home she retreated into silence, and I realized she was as worried as I was.

"When we arrived at the house, Mom thanked Slim, then caught him completely off guard by kissing him on the cheek. While she carried baby Joan and urged four-year-old Benjy inside, I removed the two dollars I owed Slim from my purse. He refused any remuneration, saying he'd enjoyed our company and was glad he was able to help.

"'At least keep one dollar for the gasoline,' I said, my

eyes suddenly watering. I guess I had my dad's pride. I hated having to take charity.

"He seemed to sense it, because he pocketed the silver dollar. 'Fair enough,' he said. 'I'll be glad to drive you or your mom up there any time. Just tell me when.'

"Mom's depression had rubbed off on me. We were all trying so hard, but things weren't getting better. I went around the side of the house to the backyard to check out our garden. That was another problem. We'd planted tomatoes and okra, squash, snap beans, English peas and bell peppers, only to have them destroyed in a hailstorm just as they were starting to bloom. We'd been counting on that garden patch to help put food on the table over the summer. Mom planned to can the excess for the winter. A few carrots, beets and onions had survived, but we couldn't live on them.

"The dollar Slim hadn't accepted might be enough to buy an old stewing hen tomorrow, which Mom could use to make chicken and dumplings. We'd be able to stretch that to last several days.

"The following morning I asked Miss Hattie if she had any other work I could do for her, maybe cleaning or washing or even cooking, if they had favorite foods they'd like me to prepare.

"She already had Elmo mopping and dusting the common areas. The girls were responsible for their own rooms, which were so small it didn't take them ten minutes a day to maintain. As for food, they could put in special requests whenever they wanted to the lunch-room two doors down that delivered their daily meals.

"I decided I'd have to keep asking around Santa Rita in the afternoons for more sewing. Anything extra I earned I'd send to the sanitarium.

"The middle of my third week Miss Hattie asked me if I'd found any other sources of income. I hadn't.

"'A few gentlemen have been inquiring about you, Evvie. They're interested.'

"I felt my face grow hot. I'd noticed the way some of them had given me the once-over, and in every case I'd quickly turned away.

"'If you really want to earn more money,' Hattie said, 'I'd be happy to hire you as one of my girls.'"

Chapter 6

"I can't deny I'd thought about what it would be like to work for Miss Hattie," Evvie went on, "but I told myself it was nothing more than curiosity, not desire. The truth is, I envied the girls at times. They seemed to have such an easy life, spending most of their day—at least when I was there—reading magazines, painting their nails, listening to Rudy Vallee on the radio and generally loafing around. They didn't have to worry about the rent or where they were going to get their next meal. I knew some of them, Miss Goldie in particular, had savings accounts in the bank next door. Her ambition, she told me, was to one day own her own bordello.

"My immediate answer to Miss Hattie was a resounding no. It had to be. First, as much as I liked the girls, I still considered what they were doing to be sinful. There was also another reason. One I didn't tell Miss Hattie about.

"'That's up to you,' she said. 'I thought since you needed money for your family you might consider it. You could be earning at least five times what you're making now.' She turned and walked away.

"Twenty-five dollars a week! We were surviving—barely—on less than fifty dollars a month.

"Even if I had been interested, how would I ever explain the sudden cash windfall to my mother? Or the strange hours I'd be working? Would I be able to go home at night? I couldn't abandon my family, and even with extra money coming in, my mother would still need help with the kids and someone to talk to.

"There was a bigger problem, too, one that scared me to death.

"I was still a virgin.

"Two days later, I was ready to leave and make my rounds of Santa Rita, when Miss Hattie called me into her parlor.

"'Have you thought any more about my offer?'

"I hung my head. In fact I'd been thinking of nothing but.

"'You don't understand,' I mumbled. 'I've never…'

"She nodded and I realized she knew exactly what I was talking about. 'I have someone in mind, someone very gentle who will help you.'

"I raised my head and was discomfited to find her looking directly at me. I bit my lip, embarrassed. 'I...can't.'

"'You're the breadwinner at home,' she said, 'and that's a big responsibility for a girl your age, but you're also old enough to understand we have to do things we don't always want to do or don't believe we can do. You have to decide which is more important, Evvie—other people's opinions of you or feeding your family.'

"Again she walked away, leaving me to fret all weekend.

"That Friday afternoon, Benjy, the four-year-old, got sick and we had to call a doctor. This was back in the days when they still made house calls. An office visit would have cost us two dollars, but we didn't have a car. It was three blocks to the city bus line, and there was no telling how long we would have to wait for a bus. The fare was a nickel apiece for us each way. Benjy's temperature was almost a hundred and three. We had no choice. I went to the neighbor next door, who had a telephone, dialed the doctor's office and told the nurse what was wrong and begged for the doctor to come as soon as possible.

"He didn't arrive until almost two hours later. He took Benjy's temperature, examined his tongue and throat, listened to his heart and lungs. He closed his little black bag. No fancy drugs. No antibiotics. He pre-scribed an aspirin every four hours and told us to keep bathing the boy with cool compresses to try to bring down his fever and to call him in the morning. If the fever went any higher during the night or he began having seizures, we were to bring him to the hospital immediately.

"Mom went to the Quaker oatmeal box where she kept the household money and counted out three dollars to pay him.

"The rent was due the following week. Mom and I had gone without food a few times, but we'd never fallen behind in the rent. We'd be in even worse shape if we did. The landlord wouldn't evict us immediately, but we'd heard of too many cases where the first default led to the second and the third until the family was unable to catch up. Then they got tossed out into the street with all their possessions—unless the landlord confiscated them for back rent.

"Mom and I spelled each other that night, washing Benjy down with wet cloths. I couldn't stop wondering what was going to happen to us. Suppose Benjy didn't recover. Suppose this was the beginning of infantile paralysis, which was a terrible scourge back in those days before the Salk vaccine. Suppose he had to go into the hospital. And what would happen if they sent Dad home?

"Benjy's fever broke the next morning, but I still couldn't sleep much the next two nights.

"I kept reviewing our options.

"Our rent was twenty dollars a month. We might have been able to find a cheaper place, but not in a part of city that was as convenient to downtown or as safe as the one we were in. What's more, we'd have to pay someone to move us.

"Our utilities—we only had gas and electric, no telephone—were another three dollars a month, and we were spending an average of another six dollars a week for food, most of it was for the baby and her four-year-old brother. Mom and I could go hungry, but they couldn't.

"Total household expenses for the month—around fifty dollars without putting any money aside for clothes, shoes or medical costs. It also didn't include sending anything to the McKnight Sanitarium for Dad.

"Mom was earning between four and five dollars a week taking in laundry. I was fetching about the same. That brought our income to around forty dollars a month—or less. Henry was sending two or three dollars a week from California. He always promised to send more, but there had been a couple of weeks when he hadn't been able to send anything. So, even though Mom and I sometimes went hungry, we were barely breaking even, and there were always unexpected expenses, like Benjy getting sick.

"I also knew I couldn't count on a steady stream of work at Miss Hattie's, because I'd already done just about everything they needed me to do.

"On Monday morning I knocked on her open door. I'm sure she understood why I was there, even before I said anything.

"Embarrassed, wringing my hands, I reminded her about what she'd said, that she had... I stopped. I couldn't get the words out. *Someone who would initiate me.*

"'You already know him,' she stated gently.

"I raised my head. 'Who?'

"'Slim.'

"My stomach flipped. With dread or relief? I couldn't say. I certainly wasn't physically attracted to him, but I did like him. He'd been kind to me and my mother. The decision I was making was a sickening one, and I was scared, as scared as I'd ever been in my entire life. The mention of his name made me feel a little better, though. I reckoned I could trust him.

"They say we never forget the first time. I haven't. It happened later that same afternoon.

"I'd seen pictures in books of Greek and Roman statues of naked men, but in most cases the private parts were either mutilated or covered. I often wondered how they got those fig leaves to stay in place. I'd never actually seen a real live naked man before. I'd most assuredly never seen one with an erection. So when I saw Slim's, it scared the daylights out of me. Surely he wasn't going to put that big...

"My girlfriends in school had been right. It hurt. I closed my eyes, bit my lips, winced with pain, shed tears and loathed myself, convinced I deserved to suffer for the terrible choice I had made. Still, the experience wasn't as completely horrible as I'd expected. Miss Hattie had been wise in choosing Slim. It wasn't until much later, after I'd been with other men, that I realized how gentle and patient he'd been. He took his time. He didn't rush or force me, and he kept assuring me I was doing fine.

"That Monday morning I'd gone to Miss Hattie's a

virgin. When I left late that afternoon, I'd crossed a bridge, one I could never double back over."

Sarah was silent for a long minute as she stared pensively out over the tawny, sun-drenched prairie.

"I crossed my own bridge, too," she finally said, "or at least, started over one the morning I picked up the money my *date* had left. Except I didn't know it at the time. My initial request for payment from the guy had been nothing more than a lark, because I wasn't planning to go to bed with him. Then, after I did, I sort of regarded it as...I don't know...a compliment? What's the difference between getting a box of chocolates or a bouquet of flowers the morning after having sex with a guy and an envelope stuffed with hundred-dollar bills? Answer—a lot. But I didn't realize it then, or maybe I just didn't want to acknowledge it."

She poured herself more liqueur and took a larger mouthful than she had previously.

"Another difference between you and me, Evvie, is that I wasn't a virgin. I'd had my first experience as a high-school senior with a football player I'd been dating for several months. I didn't consider myself loose in college, but I wasn't chaste, either."

Evvie said nothing, aware the young woman was both embarrassed by her admission and soul-searching, something that has to be done in private. Several minutes passed without either of them speaking. Cattle roamed restlessly, no doubt seeking sweeter grass in a far pasture.

"Did you get paid for your first time?" Sarah finally asked.

"Oh, yes. Slim placed the token Miss Hattie had sold him on the bedside table after he got dressed.

"'You did great,' he assured me. Gazing down at my tearstained face, he leaned over and gave me a peck on my lips. 'I hope you'll have me again. It'll be better next time,' he said."

"Did you have an..." Sarah didn't finish.

"An orgasm?" Evvie chuckled. "My, no. That wouldn't occur for some time yet. Slim left the room and I heard mumbling outside the door. A moment later Miss Hattie walked in without knocking. 'You all right?' she asked.

"I nodded. She tossed the robe from the back of the door across the bed. I had the sheet pulled up to my neck, embarrassed, ashamed that I was totally naked under it.

"'I've drawn you a warm bath,' she said. 'Then we'll talk.'

"Years before, Miss Hattie had installed one of the first bathtubs with hot and cold running water in San Angelo. I stayed in it until it was practically frigid. She'd brought my street clothes and placed them on the nearby chair. I got dressed and found her waiting for me outside when I emerged. We went to her private parlor across the hall.

"I quickly learned I was joining a business. She laid down the rules. No drinking. No cursing or foul language. I'd also have to dress more stylishly and learn to wear makeup properly. She would loan me the money for those things and deduct it from my earnings gradually.

"On the other hand, she explained, I had the right to refuse to perform acts I found unacceptable, whether they were perpetrated on me or on him. I was so naive. I had no concept of the sadomasochistic fetishes that some men found erotic pleasure in and that some women were happy to indulge. I never did go in for the kinky stuff."

"How much were you paid?" Sarah asked.

"That day, when I returned the token Slim had given me, Miss Hattie handed me a silver dollar."

"One dollar?" Sarah was outraged.

"I knew she always took half of what she charged for the girls' services and that she charged a dollar and a half for all of them except Miss Goldie, who commanded two dollars."

"So she'd charged Slim two dollars for you, too? Because you were a virgin?"

Evvie laughed. "Actually she'd charged him five for the privilege of being my first. I didn't find that out till much later, though."

Sarah snorted. "Did she make you start right away? I mean…the next day?"

"No. Miss Hattie said I needed a couple of days off to recover, emotionally, as well as physically. She was eager to have me join her girls, she said, and assured me I could earn a lot of money, but it was a big decision, and I had to consider it carefully.

"She spent the next half hour going over things I

frankly hadn't given much thought to, if any, things I didn't want to think about. Like pregnancy and venereal disease.

"She asked me about my menstrual cycle and was pleased when I told her I was very regular, very predictable. She suggested I take two days off before I expected to start my period. Most men wouldn't want me when I was bleeding. Naturally that week every month I wouldn't be earning any income, unless I was willing to give oral sex during that time. Some girls did.

"If I did become pregnant and decided I didn't want to have the baby, Miss Hattie knew a doctor who would deal with the situation for me for a modest price. The cost was my responsibility, of course. If I preferred not to go that route, I could continue to work for several months—until I became really obvious. There were a few men who were turned on by pregnant women, so I might even be able to demand a premium price from them, but there weren't many, and the decision would be completely mine.

"As for venereal disease, this was in the days before penicillin and antibiotics were available, so there weren't any surefire remedies, only things that seemed to work. Miss Hattie's reputation for running a clean house, she said, was because she had a doctor come in once a month and examine all the girls—at their expense, of course. If a girl was found to be infected, she had to leave until the episode was over and the doc approved her to return. To avoid that, she recommended I douche after each client with a vinegar-and-water solution, if I had the time. Some girls, she said, swore by other things, seltzer, Coca-Cola, even whiskey, but she wasn't really sure if they were any more effective."

"So it was strictly business," Sarah commented with disgust.

"What else could it be?" Evvie asked. "I longed desperately to talk to somebody, to unburden myself, but I couldn't tell my mother what I was doing. It would have broken her heart, which only added to my guilt. If my brother had been home I might have discussed it with him. He would have understood, even if he didn't approve, and I was certain he wouldn't, but he was far away.

"I didn't have any close friends in San Angelo. No one I could trust with this. So I kept it all bottled up inside. I spent the next two days going from house to house, begging for sewing work. I earned only seventy-five cents in those two days, and I guess that helped me reach my decision. On Thursday morning I went back to Miss Hattie's and asked her to add me to her roster."

Chapter 7

"I spent the next week apprenticed to Slim," Evvie continued. "He tutored me beyond the missionary position and clued me in on the things a girl could do to please a man. Again I was reminded of how naive I was. I'd daydreamed about sex, but in my fantasies I'd always been the focus of my erotic thoughts. Now I had to shift my attention to my partner and act solely for his pleasure. I have to admit some of what Slim asked me to do bothered me, but he never forced, only encouraged, and I soon learned to cope with and hide my revulsion. Miss Hattie reminded me I was a courtesan and part of my allure involved feigning reactions and emotions I didn't feel.

"Slim's coaching brought an unexpected complication. He'd been one of Mable's regulars and to her way of thinking I'd stolen him from her. She wasn't happy about it and didn't hesitate to voice her displeasure to Miss Hattie. As compensation Miss Hattie promised to steer more clients her way. Since we were in business to make money, Mable couldn't really complain, but I got the impression she missed Slim's company. I can't say I blamed her. He may not have been much to look at, but he was a nice guy, a regular fella, as we used to say.

"It was during the second week of my apprenticeship that the inevitable finally happened. One of Mom's church ladies told her I'd been seen by a deliveryman coming down the back stairs of Miss Hattie's bordello. She stood in the doorway of my room and demanded an explanation.

"I'd brought home ten dollars the previous week. Keep in mind the minimum wage then was thirty cents an hour, but it applied only to government jobs and corporations engaged in interstate commerce. Most local businesses didn't pay more than twenty-five cents an hour, which was perfectly legal. It was also what I'd told my mother the wealthy lady in Santa Rita was paying me. I considered repeating the lie and insisting her busybody friend from church was mistaken or it was a onetime visit because I didn't understand the nature of the place, but I'd only be delaying the inevitable. Besides, I needed to unburden myself.

"I put aside the old dress I'd purchased from Miss Goldie and was in the process of altering to fit me.

"'It's true, Mom.'

"She stared at me, confusion in her eyes. 'Are you sewing for her?'

"'I was.'

"'So it hasn't been someone in Santa Rita you've been sewing for, but that woman?'

"I closed my eyes and nodded.

"'I'm disappointed in you, Evvie. Disappointed you would even go to a place like that. Disappointed you would lie to me. We brought you up better.'

"Tears began to fall.

"'Why are you crying, Evvie? You made a mistake, but it's not that bad.'

"I broke down into racking sobs. She sat on the bed next to me and put her arm around my shoulders. 'It's only sewing, honey,' she said almost lightheartedly. 'It's not as if—'

"It finally sank in. 'Oh my God, Evvie.' She jumped up and stood in front of me, wringing her hands. 'Don't tell me! You haven't... no. No. You couldn't. Evvie. Evvie, no. Tell me it isn't true. You haven't—'

"I nodded and hung my head. I couldn't face her. I was too ashamed.

"Rather than burst into a rage, she covered her face with her hands and sank again onto the bed in a convulsion of crying. I ached to be able to soothe her, to assure her, but how? I'd become exactly what she was afraid to call me. A whore.

"'How could you?' she kept repeating. 'How could you violate the most sacred moral values we've tried to instill in you? Jesus——' she swore for the only time I ever heard her do so.

"'Don't ever tell your father. Oh, God. It'll kill him. It's killing me.' She wiped her face, or tried to. 'Does Henry know?'

"I shook my head.

"'Don't tell him, either. He has enough to contend with without learning his sister has become a Jezebel, a slut.'

"It was her way of striking out, of hurting me, and she succeeded. I loved my big brother. I loved my father. My greatest desire was to please both of them, to make them proud of me. I saw now that would never happen. I'd gone beyond the pale, betrayed their honor, as well as my own. My father and brother would never love me again. No one would.

"My mother said she couldn't accept the money I was earning by my foul sin, but she stopped short of ordering me out of the house. I was afraid that wasn't far off.

"I cried myself to sleep that night, woke up a couple of hours later and cried some more. My mother said nothing the next morning. I could see by her red-rimmed, bloodshot eyes she hadn't slept, either.

"While she washed clothes, I tried weeding the garden we'd replanted, but I couldn't concentrate, couldn't focus through my tears. When I pulled up one of the young pepper seedlings we'd just planted, I finally gave up, gathered the dress I'd been altering, left the house and trudged to Miss Hattie's. On the way I wondered if I would ever again be welcomed in my mother's house, or if now I was, like the other prostitutes at Miss Hattie's, a permanent social outcast.

"I learned that day I was a better actress than I'd ever imagined and decided maybe acting should have been my calling, because I turned six tricks that afternoon and evening, giggled, cooed and moaned at all the appropriate times, never letting the men bouncing on top of me know I felt nothing, that I was dying inside. I would have taken on six more if they had been available. *Bring them all on,* I shouted in my mind. *I don't give a damn.*

"*Money,* I told myself. *It's all about money.* The humiliation of being violated, of being used, of spawning the revulsion on my mother's face, didn't count for anything. Neither did my self-loathing, my irredeemable shame.

"It was all about putting food on the table.

"Miss Hattie stopped by my room after my last john had left.

"'What's wrong, Evvie? What's bothering you?'

"I should have realized she'd see right through my act. I told her.

"She didn't offer any sympathy, as I thought she would.

"'Stay here for a few nights,' she said. 'Give your mother time to adjust, then go home, fix the two of you a cup of tea or coffee or whatever you drink. Tell her you love her. If she refuses to accept the money you're earning, tell her she's making your sacrifice worthless.' Hattie put her hand on mine. 'She sounds like a good woman, a loving mother. Give her a chance to prove it. I think you'll be surprised.' She walked away.

"I followed her advice, with one exception. It was the middle of June, too hot for coffee or tea, so I stopped off on the way home, picked up lemons, sugar and a piece of ice and fixed a pitcher of lemonade. Nothing was more refreshing on a summer's day than the cool tang of homemade lemonade. I carried the tray to the backyard, where the washtub stood on a wooden platform, and set it on the steps of the porch.

"'I know you're disappointed in me, Mom,' I said, 'that you're ashamed of me, but will you listen to what I have to say? Will you let me explain? Please? After I've finished, if you want me to leave I will.'

"She refused to look at me, but after a moment she sat down wearily, dangling her hands, raw and red from the brown lye soap she used, between her knees and gazed at the ground. I'm sure in her heart she was convinced she was to blame for the terrible choice I'd made.

"I started off by telling her how much I loved her and Dad, that I respected all the sacrifices they'd made for Henry and me and were making for Benjy and his baby sister. Now it was time for me to make a sacrifice. I explained what I was doing wasn't because I wanted to or because I enjoyed it. I assured her I didn't. I was doing it because I didn't see any alternative. I took her chapped hands and kissed them. The gesture caught her completely by surprise. She tried to pull them away, but I wouldn't let her.

"'You're doing your best, Mom. No one could ask more. It isn't Dad's fault he's sick or that we have two extra, hungry children to feed. It isn't Henry's fault he can't send more money home. I know he's doing his best, and I love him for it.'

"'Everyone's trying as hard as they can, Mom, but it just isn't enough. Benjy's over his fever, but he's still not completely well. The hospital will admit him to the charity ward if we have to take him there, but what if it turns out to be polio? He could be crippled for the rest of his life. He's an innocent child. He doesn't deserve to suffer. And what about Dad? He isn't well enough to come home yet, and he might never be strong enough to work.'

"I let her hands slip from mine and expected her to argue with me, but she didn't.

"'Please don't hate me, Mama,' I pleaded. 'If you do, what I've sacrificed will all be in vain.'

"A moment passed, then she threw her arms around me and the two of us cried on each other's shoulders for what seemed like an eternity.

"'I'm worried about you,' she confessed a few minutes later as we attempted to sip our lemonade past the lumps in our throats. 'What you're doing is dangerous.'

"'I'll be careful,' I promised.

"We made our peace. After that I slept at Miss Hattie's Tuesday through Saturday nights and at home Sunday and Monday nights, but I also came by the house every morning, brought food, money, other things and helped Mom with the kids for as long as I could before I had to walk back to Miss Hattie's, change into my working clothes and wait for my first customer.

"As the pretty, new girl and the youngest in Miss

Hattie's stable I was in high demand. Some men preferred more experienced partners, but…well, I don't think I have to repeat the terms they used to describe me. I was a novelty and Hattie continued to charge two dollars for my services. My income skyrocketed. Soon I was able to buy new clothes and shoes for the growing kids and send money to Carlsbad."

"How many…"

"Tricks did I turn?" Evvie finished for her.

Sarah shifted uneasily and nodded.

"It varied from day to day and the time of the month." She smiled. "I'm referring to paydays, Sarah, not my cycle. During the middle of the week, I might have as few as three or four clients a day. On Friday and Saturday nights it would be at least double that, and if the last day of the month fell on a weekend, I might have ten or fifteen customers a day."

"But you said there weren't many jobs," Sarah said. "Who could afford to go to Miss Hattie's? My clients were all well-heeled guys who thought nothing of five-hundred-dollar-a-night hotel suites in addition to my fees. Businessmen mostly, some of them from out of town, but occasionally there were athletes, a few academics, even an occasional man of the cloth. Then there were guys who did nothing for a living, except spend money."

"Ah, the leisure class," Evvie said with a snort. "We had them back then, too." She tightened and loosened her hands to work out the arthritic stiffness. "Not everyone was living hand-to-mouth, my dear. A few ranchers had money, though most were land rich and cash poor. Ranch hands didn't get paid much, but they didn't spend much, either, and some of them, especially if they didn't have families to support, made a trip to Miss Hattie's part of their monthly visits to town. Businessmen, like bankers and oilmen, did quite well. Then there were, as you say, clergymen and teachers. I don't remember any athletes, but they weren't paid as well back then as they are nowadays—though we did a land-office business when the rodeo was in town. A few military people, too."

"Can I ask how much you would make, say, in a month? On average?" Sarah asked a little sheepishly.

"Remember, I only worked three weeks out of four, and if my off week happened to be when payday hit, I took a big loss. On average, though, I was making about forty dollars a week before deductions."

"Deductions for what?"

Evvie smiled. "Well, there was the medical exam every month. That was five dollars. Linen and laundry service and the meals that were delivered, another fifteen. Personal toiletries and cosmetics I had to buy, a couple more bucks a week. Someone already established—Miss Goldie, for instance, who was willing to do just about anything for a buck and who rarely took time off—was probably clearing closer to sixty dollars a week. We're talking at least three thousand dollars a year, when the average annual income for a breadwinner was about nineteen hundred."

"How about Miss Hattie?" Sarah asked. "How much was she making?"

"I don't know for sure, but I figure she was probably grossing between nine and ten thousand a year. Of course, she had expenses we didn't have, such as bribing the right people—and there were plenty of them. Cops, judges, city councilmen. Even if she was only netting five thousand a year, she was in high cotton."

Chapter 8

As they sat in the café drinking coffee, Edgar gazed out the window at the traffic moving slowly through the intersection, at the pedestrians strolling along the sidewalk or waiting for the light to change. Mostly tourists. In the old days they would have been businessmen and household shoppers, except that by one o'clock on Saturday most merchants would have shut down for the weekend.

A different lifestyle then. Different priorities. But different values?

He looked at his grandson sitting across from him. Handsome. Well educated. Sophisticated. How old was he? Twenty-five? He seemed so young, so untried. By that age, Edgar had been through…

Time to resume his tale.

"I was a healthy young man, and while I genuinely respected my father's calling, I didn't exactly share his virtue. I'd initially sampled the sins of the flesh five years before, found them agreeable and had indulged at regular intervals thereafter. Which was one reason I didn't want to accompany my parents to the jungles of Africa. They didn't need to be witnesses to all my vices. Anyway, the idea of visiting a house of ill repute didn't really intimidate me, as I suspect Zeke had expected it to.

"What I found on the second floor of Miss Hattie's bordello fairly well matched my expectations. Red velvety wallpaper. Victorian furniture. A sideboard with decanters of whiskey and brandy. Only one thing surprised me, or rather one person.

"A young woman, a teenager really, who absolutely knocked my socks off. Pretty. Oh, so pretty. Beautiful, in fact. With the most gorgeous green eyes I'd ever beheld. Bobbed hair was out of fashion by then. Women were wearing their hair longer, going for more natural-looking coils and waves. This gal's soft reddish-brown hair cascaded to her shoulders in a way that made a man want to run his fingers through it. She had a creamy soft complexion, and those eyes. They reminded me of fine Chinese jade.

"Yet there was another quality about her that intrigued me. It wasn't just her youth and natural beauty. I sensed a melancholy innocence about her that made me want to carry her off in my arms and protect her from the savagery of the world.

"Sir Galahad at your service.

"The really strange part, however, was that, even though I was in a house of easy virtue, lust wasn't the first thing on my mind. Okay, at nineteen it's never too far behind whatever is first, but at that moment, as I stood gazing at this beautiful gal, what I wanted more than anything was to get to know her.

"Except my reason for being there was to sell a new automobile to the madam, not sit and spoon with a girl who made me yearn to play knight-errant."

Evvie glanced over at the young woman sitting nearby. She was so pretty, so charming. Evvie had no doubt why her grandson was attracted to her, or why some men would be willing to pay for the pleasure of her company.

The two women had that in common, their illicit experience with men, but they had arrived at those experiences so differently. For Evvie they had been accompanied with moral shame and social disgrace. Her granddaughter-in-law seemed to have suffered neither. Money had been the motivating factor for Evvie. For Sarah it had only been a perk.

Different generations. Different values. Or were they? If Sarah wasn't ashamed of what she had done, why had she asked Bram to divorce her?

"One day I was sitting in the parlor, talking to a cowboy who'd just ridden into town, when I glanced over and saw a stranger at the top of the stairs. Tall, broad shouldered, he had thick, shiny jet-black hair combed straight back in the fashion of the day and the most gorgeous blue eyes I'd ever seen. His dark lashes were unbelievably long. Nowadays we'd call him drop-dead handsome. Back then we called him a dreamboat.

"He glanced over at me from the top of the stairs, one hand still on the newel post, and I felt my insides turn to Jell-O. What was this scrumptious hunk of heartbreak doing in a brothel? He most assuredly didn't need to pay a woman to go to bed with him. All he had to do was crook his finger and every female in sight, hooker or not, would come a-running.

"'Excuse me,' he said as he approached. From his accent I pegged him as not being a Texan—at least, not a West Texan. 'I'm looking for Miss Hattie.'

"I raised a shaky finger and pointed to the hallway behind him. 'Her office is through there, first door on the right.'

"He smiled and my Jell-O core melted. He had perfectly even, sparkling white teeth and a mouth that made me stare. I'd never reacted to a man that way, and I didn't know what to make of it.

"'Thank you,' he said and turned in that direction, but not before making the kind of eye contact that suggested he was thinking thoughts similar to mine. Kismet. The conjunction of two stars."

"I stood in the doorway of Miss Hattie's office. The room wasn't very big, but it was fussy, with old-fashioned furniture and lots of lace doilies. The woman behind the desk was stylishly dressed and heavily made up, but I quickly perceived that under all the cosmetics she was probably old enough to be my grandmother.

"She gazed up, and I could feel her assessing me. Cousin Zeke was emphatic that when trying to sell expensive cars to rich people, you had to be well dressed. That day I had on my best duds, a cream-colored linen suit that had been custom-made for me by a Chinese tailor a couple of years earlier as a special thanks to my parents for their kindness to his family when they were fleeing the marauding Japanese. I'd grown since then, so the trousers were a bit short, but standing in front of her desk, I didn't reckon Miss Hattie noticed. Holding my panama hat in hand I introduced myself, explained why I was there and started giving her my pitch.

"It didn't take me long to realize neither my clothes nor my charms were making much of an impression on the old dame.

"To give you an idea of what I was hustling, the 1941 Packard convertible coupe sold for about eleven hundred dollars. A basic Ford at that time cost less than seven hundred bucks, their fancy convertible coupe for about nine hundred. So I was selling a more expensive and more stylish automobile. On the other hand, Miss Hattie's '35 LaSalle, which was what they called a companion car to the Cadillac—that is, a less expensive line—was no longer in production. The Cadillac convertible coupe, however, was available at around sixteen-fifty. Remember, this is at a time when the average income—for people who had jobs—was less than two thousand a year.

"She asked a few predictable questions, but crafty businesswoman that she was, she held her cards close to her chest. I couldn't tell if she was interested in the Packard or not.

"That was all right. It afforded me an excuse to come by again to remind her of the tremendous bargain I was peddling—and get another gander at that pretty gal in the parlor."

"'Miss Evvie.'

"I started, only then realizing the guy I was sitting with was addressing me. I turned to the cowboy and wondered where this wart-faced frog had materialized from, though only a minute earlier I'd found him pleasant enough.

"'Can we go now?' he asked, clearly annoyed with the interruption.

"'Oh, sure.' I clutched his hand and led him back to my room.

"Later—I don't think he lasted very long—I saw him out the back door and glanced in the sitting room to see if anyone was there before stopping by Miss Hattie's office.

"'Where'd that fella go?' I didn't specify who I meant, and I refused to believe he'd been there to buy sex. 'What did he want, anyway?'

"'Car salesman,' she muttered absentmindedly as she accepted the token the cowboy had given me, put it in her top drawer and flipped to my page in her ledger so she could give me credit for it.

"'Are you going to buy a new car?' I thought her shiny LaSalle was one of the smartest automobiles in town.

"'I'm considering it. He's been showing me the new Packard convertible coupe.' We pronounced it coupé. 'I have to admit it's a nifty-looking roadster.'

"'What's his name?'

"She shifted her eyes to me. I wasn't usually this inquisitive. 'Edgar Clyburn.'

"'Mmm,' I mumbled as though I had suddenly lost interest.

"Just then I recognized the sound of male feet bounding up the staircase two at a time. A moment later he barged into the room but stopped short inside the doorway when he saw me.

"'I brought you these brochures,' he said to Miss Hattie, though his eyes kept flicking to me. He snapped his fingers. 'I have an even better idea. Why don't I take you for a test drive. That way you'll get a feel for how that baby handles. It's a real beaut. You'll love it.'

"'You can go, Evvie,' Miss Hattie said quietly to me.

"I turned to the doorway, but the big tall visitor was blocking it, and he made no move to get out of my way.

"'Why not bring her along?' he told Miss Hattie. 'You'll be impressed with the horsepower of the silky-smooth straight eight, and Miss…Evvie?…here can give you her opinion of the suspension as a passenger.'

"I liked the sound of his voice, deep and mellow, and

he talked with a kind of confidence and sophistication that made me want to just stand there and listen to his every word.

"'Maybe another time,' Miss Hattie responded, and I could tell she was annoyed. 'Leave those with me.' She motioned to the folder in his right hand. 'I'll give them a gander when I have a chance.'

"I couldn't help staring at him as he stepped forward and spread out a series of glossy pictures and other papers on her desk. He had large hands, strong hands. I couldn't drag my eyes off them. Miss Hattie glared in my direction, and I was forced to move out into the hall.

"A minute later the visitor emerged, smiled and nodded to me, pronounced my name and went back down the stairs.

"Miss Hattie had invited him to come back in a few days. I sure hoped I was around when he did. Clark Gable and Gary Cooper wrapped in one. With a touch of Jimmy Stewart's boyishness thrown in for good measure. A real heartthrob. I'd never encountered anyone like him.

"He showed up the next afternoon. Of course he was familiar with where Miss Hattie's office was now, so he didn't have to ask directions, but he didn't go straight there. Instead he sauntered over to the settee, where I was paging through the latest issue of *Collier's* magazine, stood in front of me and said, 'Hi, my name's Edgar Clyburn.' Which, of course, I already knew.

"I almost said Evvie Douglas, but stopped in time. Miss Hattie didn't approve of us giving out our last names. Not that people couldn't find out what they were if they really tried. It was just a way of maintaining privacy. 'Hi.'

"'Do you mind if I sit down, Miss Evvie?'

"So he remembered my name. I tried hard to be nonchalant, all the time wondering if he could see my hand trembling with excitement as I waved him to the cushion beside me. 'Be my guest. Where are you from, Mr. Clyburn?'

"'Call me Edgar. Nowhere special,' he said. 'I was born in St. Louis, but I've never lived there.'

"'Why not?'

"'My dad's a missionary. We moved around a lot.'

"The son of a missionary. I almost laughed. He wouldn't be the first man of the cloth or son of a preacher to tarry at Miss Hattie's to unburden himself of the temptations of the flesh.

"'Where do you live now?' I asked.

"'Here in San Angelo. Nice town.'

"'Do you have family here?'

"'My cousin Zeke. He owns a car dealership. I work for him. I'll be glad to sell you a car…or a tractor, if that's what you want.'

"I laughed. 'No thanks. We don't have a farm anymore.'

"'You used to?' He obviously wanted to chat, and so did I.

"'Mr. Clyburn,' Miss Hattie said sharply. The room wasn't that big and there was no one else around, yet she'd managed to sneak up on both of us. 'I told you to give me a few days to think the matter over.'

"He jumped up. 'I...I thought I'd stop by to see if you had any questions. The coupe comes with whitewalls, and it's available with leather seats in black, white or tan.'

"'You told me that yesterday.'

"'Oh.' He stuffed his hands in his pockets. 'I just thought...'

"'I have your card, Mr. Clyburn. If I think of anything, I'll ring you at your office.'

"'Um, uh, well, yeah, sure. Thank you.' He started toward the staircase. 'If you have any question at all—'

"'Goodbye, Mr. Clyburn.'

"'Call me Edgar,' he said and raised a hand to me. 'Swell meeting you, Evvie.'

"I waved back. 'Swell meeting you, too, Edgar.'

"Miss Hattie waited until she heard the downstairs door close. 'He doesn't have to buy, Evvie, and he's not going to, so don't waste your charms on him.'

"For the first time I felt real anger at Miss Hattie. She'd always been nice to me, in a distant sort of way, but now she was reminding me that men were interested in me for just one thing, that I wasn't good enough for nice guys like Edgar Clyburn. She made me ashamed, and she made me angry—at her and at myself.

"I wanted to tell her she didn't have to run him off, that maybe he liked talking to me, that I liked talking to him, but sassing her wouldn't be smart. I needed her a lot more than she needed me. She could always find another whore to take my place. The men who gave me their tokens didn't care about me or what my name was.

"He didn't show up the next day, and that put me in a foul mood. I snapped at one of my johns when he didn't get a move on and ended up having to offer him a bonus to keep him from tattling on me to Miss Hattie. Three complaints and she would keep an extra share of my fee or send my clients to one of the other girls. I couldn't afford that.

"Edgar finally showed up the following Wednesday. His face instantly brightened when we made eye contact, and we started chatting like two old friends who hadn't seen each other in ages. Again I got so distracted by his good looks and the funny story he was telling me that I didn't notice Miss Hattie walk up behind him. We both jumped when she spoke.

"'I've thought about the coupe,' she said. 'It's a fine-looking automobile, Mr. Clyburn, and you've made me a tempting offer, but I'm not in the market for a new car right now. Maybe next year.'

"'It's much more economically priced than the new Cadillac,' he reminded her. 'We'll give you a very generous trade-in on your old car. The Packard is equipped with a swell new radio,' he rambled on, not nearly as smooth talking as he had been with me a minute earlier. 'Did I tell you we'll throw in free car washes for a year? The dealership is very close. Or if that's not convenient for you, you can call me and I'll be happy to pick up the car and deliver it back to you when it's ready. It's the top of the line—'

"'No,' she said firmly and with unmistakable finality. 'Thank you for coming, Mr. Clyburn.'

"He glanced at me, and I could see he didn't want to leave any more than I wanted him to.

"He drew a deep breath, and I noticed again how broad his chest was. 'Um, would it be all right if I visited with Miss Evvie for a few minutes?'

"Hattie studied me, then frowned at him. 'She has paying customers to attend to,' she said.

"It felt like a slap, especially since at that moment it wasn't true. No one was waiting. Lowering my head to hide my shame, I fought back tears.

"'Should you decide to drop by again,' she told him pointedly, 'I'll expect you to pay for Miss Evvie's time.' She stepped aside for him to leave. 'Good day, Mr. Clyburn.'

"Too humiliated to meet his eyes, I nevertheless couldn't help glancing up. His face was red and a vein in his neck was pulsing.

"Miss Hattie crossed her arms like a haughty schoolmarm, waiting for him to leave.

"'It was a pleasure talking to you, Evvie.' He walked leisurely over to the staircase and unhurriedly descended the steps.

"I glanced at the woman who'd brought me to where I was. 'Why did you do that?' I protested, surprising myself by my audacity. 'He wasn't doing any harm.'

"'For your own good,' she declared without an ounce of pity or remorse. 'Don't get any illusions about who you are or what your role is here, Evvie. This isn't a wedding chapel. It's a whorehouse. If you want hearts and flowers, you'll have to go elsewhere.' She paused only a moment. 'If you think I'm being unreasonable, talk to Rosie. She'll set you straight.'

"I cried myself to sleep that night. What would become of me? Would I ever get the chance to meet someone who was interested in me as a person, as a woman, not just as a bought-and-paid-for piece of ass? What about marriage and a family? Was I doomed to grow old alone, to end up a diseased harlot with a painted face?"

Chapter 9

Edgar looked up as the waitress came by the table to refill their coffee cups.

"Was that carrot cake I saw behind the counter?" he asked.

"Yes, sir. Real good, too. Homemade."

"In that case, bring me a piece. Bram, you want some?"

His grandson shook his head and the waitress left. "Where do you get the room? After that big lunch we had—"

Edgar patted his flat belly. "Blessed with a cast-iron stomach and a hearty appetite. In Asia they judge a man's capacity by the number of bowls of rice he eats at one sitting. I was a three-bowl man myself. Now, where was I?"

Bram studied him. "Gramps, what you're telling me is unbelievable. I mean… You're saying Gram was a…"

"She was a working girl, son. The prettiest one in the whole darn place."

"But— Why did she…?"

"Turn tricks? Because her family was hungry."

Bram shook his head. "But… Surely… There must have been other alternatives. I mean—"

Edgar cut him off. "You've lived a pretty cushy life. I don't begrudge it to you. I wish everyone could receive a brand-new car as a high-school graduation present, go to a first-rate college on an athletic scholarship, wear expensive clothes, take cruises in the Caribbean and go skiing in the Alps, but not everyone has had your advantages."

He sucked in a deep breath and willed his blood pressure to settle. He didn't usually get into a lather like this, but they were talking about Evvie. His Evvie. He hated what she had done, what she had been forced to do, hated the choice she'd had to make, but he had never hated her, even when he thought he did. He loved that woman. Always had. Always would.

He was proud of his grandson, too, proud of his achievements in school and in sports, pleased he had plans to expand the family business. He was even pleased he was regarded highly enough to be considered for public office.

Nonetheless, Edgar wasn't about to let the young man squint down his nose at the woman he loved.

"Before you start passing judgment on the choices other people have made, maybe you ought to find out what their circumstance were when they made them. You have absolutely no idea what it was like in 1941 or to be a woman then."

Edgar drew another breath and started to lift the cup of coffee to his lips, but his hand was shaking. He put it back down on the table.

"Damn it," he growled, though he kept his voice low, "your grandmother sacrificed her virtue and her reputation because there was no other way to put food on the table, not because she wanted a new dress or a ski vacation or because it gave her kicks."

Bram's face darkened. He tensed and turned his head away. "You're right. Excuse me for asking."

Edgar closed his eyes and opened them. "I'm sorry, son. I shouldn't have run off at the mouth like that." He paused a moment. "We all make mistakes, some for reasons we can justify, others we only rationalize. To the people who haven't been there, it really doesn't make any difference."

The waitress brought the carrot cake, a big square of it, topped with cream-cheese icing. She handed Bram a second fork. "I thought you might want to sneak a taste when he's not looking—" she refilled their coffee cups "—so you know what you're missing."

Bram gave her a wan smile. "Thanks."

She moved away.

Edgar's hand was still shaky as he picked up his fork,

but he managed to get a bite to his mouth without dropping a crumb.

"Mmm." He closed his eyes and savored the cake. "You really ought to try this," he said, as if his previous outburst hadn't happened.

Bram shook his head, watched the old man eat for a minute.

Edgar put the fork down.

"Son, I'm not telling you these things to diminish your grandmother in your eyes," he said. "I love that woman more than life itself and I'll do anything in my power to protect her. If you ever come to love your wife half as much as I love mine, you'll be the luckiest man in the world."

He mulled over what his grandfather had been telling him. "This must be what Jane Spicer was referring to when she said all our family secrets would be exposed if I dared run against her husband. You're telling me you don't want me to go into politics because someone might find out about Gram and embarrass her, but I already told you I don't—"

The old man shook his head. "No, son, I'm not worried about that. They're scare tactics to make you back off."

"But—" Bram was thoroughly confused. "Then why are you telling me all this?"

Edgar took a sip of coffee before answering.

"She won't say anything in public."

"I still don't understand, Gramps," Bram said. "Why not?"

"Because it would be actionable."

"If it's true—"

"How would she prove it? Think about it. Your grandmother is eighty-three years old. She was sixteen when she was one of Miss Hattie's girls. Every single one of her clients was older, most of them by ten years or more. Do the math. They're either dead or so ancient they'd lack reliability, even if they were willing to disclose their youthful indiscretions. Jane Spicer can't produce a single credible witness to substantiate her slanderous statements."

Bram nodded. "That still doesn't explain why you're telling me all this. I could have called her bluff without ever knowing the truth."

"She could still make the claims in private, and you'd always wonder if they might be true. Now you know."

"That's small consolation, Gramps."

The old man smiled. "Let me go on with my story."

He forked up the last morsel of carrot cake and washed it down with a mouthful of cooling coffee.

"After Miss Hattie gave me the bum's rush, I did something Cousin Zeke would have laughed his ass off at. I shelled out two hard-earned bucks for an hour of Evvie's time."

"What was this about Rosie?" Sarah asked.

Evvie refilled their cordial glasses. After taking a sip she said, "A couple of years before, Rosie had married one of her regulars. Every hooker's dream. Six months later she was back at Miss Hattie's plying her trade. The guy who'd given her a ring and made an honest woman out of her insisted he really cared for her, but after they settled down he said he couldn't get past all the other men she'd been with, especially when he found out some of them were his best friends. The lesson was unequivocal. Once a hooker, always a hooker."

Obviously that hadn't been true with Evvie and Edgar, and Sarah was eager to find out how they had worked their way past that particular hurdle, but first she had other questions.

"How did you and your mother get along after you told her what you were doing?"

"I never doubted she continued to love me, but we lost something that day, the kind of mother/daughter intimacy we'd shared before. I was willing to answer any questions she might have had about Miss Hattie's. I don't mean the sex part. She would never have asked about that, and I don't think I could have talked about it if she had, but I figured she might at least be curious about the other girls, who they were, their personalities, where they were from, their family situations. And, of course, about Miss Hattie herself. But Mom never asked a single question about any of them, never mentioned the place. After the shock of what I was doing wore off she accepted why I'd made the decision I had, but I always felt at her core she was ashamed of me."

"Did you ever tell your father?" Sarah said quietly.

"Not me, and I'm positive Mom didn't. I wondered at times if he might have heard from other sources, but that didn't seem probable. We hadn't lived in Texas long enough for him to make any close friends, and what kind of friend would tell a dying man his daughter was a whore? It must have been a terribly lonely life for him at the sanitarium, dependent on strangers, isolated from the family he loved. Because he was still contagious he hadn't even been allowed to go to his brother John's funeral. If he did find out about me, he kept it to himself. I prefer to think he never did, that he died believing I was still the innocent little girl he'd raised."

Evvie's voice didn't quaver and her eyes didn't flinch, but Sarah sensed deep sadness in the old woman's comment.

Sarah was beginning to realize she'd never truly understood the term "hard times," and it reinforced her own sense of guilt. Sarah had chosen to make disgraceful decisions out of pure selfishness.

"Whatever happened to Slim?" she asked.

Evvie smiled nostalgically. "He visited me regularly for a while, then abruptly stopped coming around. Turned out he'd met a widow lady with a couple of kids, married her and moved to Colorado. I never saw or heard from him again. I've often wondered if he found happiness. I hope so. He was at heart a good man."

"Benjy. Did he get better?"

"Recovered completely. It wasn't polio, thank God. He eventually grew into a splendid young man, went to West Point and graduated at the top of his class. He was killed in Vietnam."

"I'm sorry."

A minute passed.

"Okay," Sarah finally said, "now, tell me more about Edgar."

"Three days went by and he hadn't shown up. I was sure I would never see him again. Then I heard the front door open and the sound of a man's footsteps on the stairs. As I said, not too many of our clients came in directly from the street. Even without a sign on the door, everyone seemed to know about number eighteen and a half East Concho.

"I was sitting in the parlor at the time, idly leafing through a tattered copy of *Life* magazine, when his head appeared above the banister. My pulse did a jitterbug.

"He turned, as if sensing I was there, studied me a few seconds with those cobalt-blue eyes of his, then went down the hall. To Miss Hattie's parlor. Was he still intent on selling her that new Packard coupe? If so, he was wasting his time. Once she made up her mind, the decision might as well be cast in concrete. Pestering her would only put him on her bad side.

"He reappeared a minute later, and I figured she'd told him to amscray, but he walked past the staircase and stood directly in front of me. I expected him to tell me he had to go. Instead he beamed a bashful smile and held out his hand, palm up. In it was a token.

"I couldn't figure out what to make of it. He was

buying my favors. Because I was available and he was horny? Or because he had the hots for me personally? Neither alternative was particularly appealing. Oh, I wouldn't have minded giving him a bounce, but it disappointed me, even hurt, that he, too, had reduced me to what I was. Any of the other girls could have provided the same service. Besides, once a fella got the rhythm going, he didn't know—or care—who was under him.

"I didn't meet his eyes when I relieved him of the token. I didn't even offer my hand as I started to lead him down the hall to my room. He surprised me when he took mine and held it, as though...as though I meant something to him.

"Some of my johns had hands that were as soft as a woman's. Others were coarse and callused from manual labor. Edgar's hand...well, it was warm, and as comfortable as fine leather. Which didn't help matters.

"I was angry, disappointed, insulted. I'd sensed something different, something special, when I'd been with Edgar on his previous visits. Now he'd spoiled everything. I'd felt cheap with other men, but walking down the hall with him that afternoon I felt worthless, like a piece of disposable merchandise. I loathed him, and I loathed myself.

"When we arrived at my room, I reached out for the handle of the screen door, but he was ahead of me and held it open for me, stood aside to let me precede him. A real gentleman.

"I went in. He followed. I pulled down the shade

to furnish us privacy. Turning around, I started to unbutton the bodice of my cotton dress.

"He cupped his hands around mine, his fingers not quite making contact with my breasts, but I was distinctly aware of their heat.

"He shook his head. 'I just want to talk, Evvie,' he said softly. That caught my breath and darn near made me cry.

"The men who patronized me were there for only one thing, and it wasn't conversation. Most of them were in a hurry to get down to business and be on their way, which was fine with me. Only rarely did I have a client who demonstrated a need for social foreplay, usually one of the younger fellas who were there for the first time and were nervous as hell. I'd quickly learned how to, shall we say, stroke their egos so we could get on with it.

"'Sure,' I said. 'Whatever you want.'

"My room consisted of an iron double bed, a chifforobe with two drawers on the bottom, a marble-topped bedside stand, a straight-back cane-bottom chair next to it for me to drape my clothes on and a similar one in the corner at the foot of the bed for my guest's things. Neither chair was particularly comfortable to sit on, but then, they weren't intended for that purpose.

"I was about to park my haunches on the side of the mattress, when he crooked a finger under my chin and raised my head compelling me to look at him.

"'That's all, Evvie. Miss Hattie said I had to pay her to spend time with you, so that's what I did. I just want to talk, to get to know you better.'

"I was stunned.

"He motioned for me to sit on the bed, while he pulled over a chair and straddled it, facing me.

"I don't remember exactly how we got started, though I'm sure it was a little awkward at first. I wasn't used to carrying on an intelligent conversation with a man—not there, at least. Exchanging pleasantries, sure. Laughing at their cute, ribald, tasteless and occasionally insulting remarks, yeah, but have a real exchange of ideas? Wow! It was a new experience for me. I'd been too young to date when we lived in Oklahoma, and I hadn't been in school in Texas long enough to make friends. Not boyfriends. Except for Henry, I didn't have any male friends. He and I were close, but he was my brother, so he didn't count.

"That afternoon Edgar and I sat and talked for almost two hours. He asked me where I was from, how long I had been in San Angelo. What I thought of it. Questions I'd been asked before, but this time was different. Edgar was actually listening to my replies. That pleased me, but I was much more interested in hearing about him.

"He described the countries he'd lived in with his parents. Exotic places like Japan, China, India, Siam, the Philippine Islands. He recounted visits to Sumatra and Borneo. I didn't tell him I had no idea where those places were. He'd been to Africa, too, he said, when he was a little kid. He explained that his parents had recently returned there to preach the gospel of the Lord.

"I'd been brought up a Christian, so I couldn't help feeling a little intimidated about his father being an ordained minister. Was that why Edgar just wanted to talk? Did he think he was going to save me from my life of sin? Only if the Lord was going to send me twenty-five to thirty bucks a week, I mused cynically.

"Why didn't you go with your folks?" I asked.

"They're good people and I love them, but I want to live my own life."

"As we jabbered on and laughed, I realized I hadn't felt so good about myself or about being with someone, except my brother, Henry, in ages. All anybody ever seemed to talk about were problems. When was it going to rain? When would the drought end? How would we ever be able to pay our bills? Get work? Buy food? Lately Mom and I were constantly fretting about the children's health, these cousins I'd been only vaguely aware of a year earlier. Everyone said we were going through hard times, but what were good times? I couldn't remember.

"Edgar was different. He was giving me a glimpse of other worlds, of places full of excitement and adventure, of new experiences and mysterious people. Later he would tell me about the cruelty and devastation he'd seen, particularly in China at the hands of the Japanese, but for now it was all exploration and discovery. My youth had ended months before, shortly after my sixteenth birthday, but that afternoon, I was young and innocent again, carefree and happy to be with this fascinating man.

"My sense of well-being was shattered when Miss

Hattie knocked on the screen door and informed Edgar his time was up, that I had a visitor to attend to.

"Again she had crammed ugly reality, the one I despised, between us. I was mortified. My eyes burned as Edgar obediently climbed to his feet and put the chair back in its place.

"'I'll come again,' he said, adding, 'if that's all right.'

"I could only nod. He planted an affectionate kiss on my forehead, the way my brother used to, paused and brushed his hands across my shoulders and down my arms. The gleam in his beautiful blue eyes as he briefly clasped my hands was definitely not brotherly. It caught my breath. I didn't want him to ever let go.

"'Thanks for a swell time, Evvie,' he said, turned and left the room.

"I listened, heartsick, as his footsteps receded down the hall."

Chapter 10

"I'd purchased an hour of Evvie's time," Edgar said, "but I spent nearly two with her that afternoon in her tiny room. We talked. No sex. There wasn't even any touching. Just conversation. I sat mesmerized by the animation in her incredible green eyes, while she told me about herself, about the family's sad plight in Oklahoma, her brother hightailing it out to California in search of work, her dad being shut up in a TB sanitarium, her mother taking in wash to feed the family. As I listened I had a terrible, wonderful urge to gather this beautiful girl in my arms, press her head to my chest and assure her everything was going to be all right.

"She drew me out, too. Played on every young man's love of hearing himself talk, mostly about himself. I told her about my travels with my parents, the places I'd lived and visited. The way she seemed to hang on to my every word made me feel like a combination of worldly adventurer and wise man. Before we knew it, Miss Hattie was knocking on the door informing me it was time for me to skedaddle. Naturally I was disappointed that I had to leave, but I didn't get mad until Miss Hattie made a point of adding that Evvie had other paying customers waiting.

"It was a sucker punch to the gut or lower, and it made my blood boil. Evvie's face turned red, as though she'd been slapped. Humiliated, she lowered her head. More than ever, I had this hankering to take her into my arms.

"I've never hit a woman, never wanted to, never could, but if Miss Hattie had been a man, I would have punched her lights out. She'd calculatedly embarrassed Evvie by reminding her and me why she was there. I didn't care to contemplate what would be transpiring on that bed after I left.

"Had I been able to, I would have picked Evvie up at that moment and carried her away in my arms. Instead I had to smother my rage and be polite or at least civil, if I was to have any hope of being allowed back.

"I kissed Evvie on the forehead, told her I'd see her again soon and left."

"I wiped my nose with a hankie," Evvie said, "but took another minute to dry my eyes, held my head up high, plastered a smile on my puss and sashayed down the corridor to meet my next caller. On the way, I passed Miss Hattie's parlor and dropped off the token Edgar had given me.

"She raised her pencil-thin eyebrows at me, as if she expected me to say something. When I didn't—I refused to give the old bat the satisfaction of knowing how much she'd hurt me—she went back to her log. Neither of us uttered a word.

"I'm sure she was aware we'd done nothing but talk. The shade on the door shielded us from prying eyes but didn't do much to muffle sounds.

"Miss Hattie's attitude was straightforward. She didn't care what customers did as long as the girl was willing and nobody got hurt. For the most part my clients and I engaged in the missionary position, but that day—for me, at least—the missionary position assumed a whole new meaning.

"During the next week I constantly relived every word Edgar had said, savored the afterglow of being with him. I pictured his smile. The way he held his head when he was considering a question I'd asked. The way he gazed off into space while he formulated an answer. Recalling the sound of his laughter as he described a funny incident he'd experienced made me feel good inside.

"Wednesday rolled around again. I was in the dining room, listening to an episode of *Stella Dallas,* an afternoon soap opera, on the radio, when I heard the tread of feet on the stairs. From habit I went to the door and looked out.

"There he was, standing at the head of the stairs. He smiled at me. My head got light and my knees grew weak. Shyly I smiled back.

"He went around the corner to Miss Hattie's office and emerged again only seconds later, holding up a token. He grinned and waited for me to join him, offered me the slug, then, laughing, grabbed my hand in his as I reached for it.

"It's hard to describe how his hand holding mine made me feel. This big, strong, gorgeous hunk, only a few years older than me. He wasn't a john, a customer I had to please. He was a friend, an ally, a person I could trust not to hurt me.

"We went back to my room. I pulled down the shade and sat on the bed. He pulled up the chair and resumed his place directly in front of me.

"This time as we talked, though, I felt something sweet stir inside me. A nervous excitement. A kind of tension that made me jumpy and anxious, yet also made me want to giggle. It was an indescribable feeling, frustrating and pleasant at the same time.

"I couldn't have explained even to myself why I invited him to sit on the bed with me, except that I wanted to be closer to him. Our eyes locked as he moved up to my side. Impulsively I reached for his hand, caressed it. I was used to physical contact with men, but not the shiver that went through me when his thigh rubbed against mine.

"'Will you kiss me, Edgar?' I asked.

"He gazed at me but didn't answer, and for a terrifying moment I was afraid I'd spoiled everything, crossed an invisible line, that this son of a preacher was going to get up and leave. Then he shifted his weight, lowered his head and brought his lips to mine.

"I don't remember him drawing me into his arms, but I do remember being there and the way he made my heart pound. We were both breathless when he finally broke off. A kiss like none I'd ever experienced. A kiss I hoped would never end.

"'You're so beautiful,' he murmured in my ear as he continued to hold me.

"I could smell the brilliantine in his hair, the light scent of witch hazel on his skin. I felt incredibly safe in his arms. I felt, too, something that had never happened to me before. Dampness between my legs.

"'Evvie,' he whispered as he stroked my back. 'Evvie…will you let me make love to you?'

"My mind plunged into a quagmire. Questions battered me. Was this what he'd been after all along—getting laid? As quickly as the thought surfaced I dismissed it. If that was all he'd wanted, he could have had it last time. Instead we'd talked. If he'd come to me this time with the intention of having sex, we needn't have gabbed for the past half hour. He could have initiated it a long time ago. Instead I'd been the one who'd invited him to sit beside me on the bed. I'd been the one who'd asked to be kissed.

"'Sure,' I said. 'That's what I'm here for.' I started to rise, so I could take off my clothes.

"'No,' he said sharply, stopping me in midmotion.

'No,' he repeated more gently. 'I don't want to have sex with you, Evvie. I want to make love with you.'

"Stupid, naive girl that I was, I had no idea what he was talking about. Having sex, screwing, humping, making love. It was all the same. Slim had been gentle and considerate, but there'd been no romance in what we'd done. A physical act, that was all, a coupling designed to please him, fulfill his desires. My reward, if I expected any besides the fee he paid, was the satisfaction of having done a good job.

"But the way Edgar said he wanted to make love *with* me suggested I was supposed to find gratification, as well. I didn't understand how that could be.

"'Why don't you take the lead,' I said, as much to hide my ignorance as to let him know he was the boss. Men couldn't resist that—to dominate. To feel superior.

"What happened over the next hour was completely new to me. He undressed me, slowly, painstakingly, touching me in ways I'd never been touched. The dampness between my legs turned to wetness and made me self-conscious, worried, shy. I felt vulnerable at the same time I found myself impatiently wanting to rip his clothes off. I kept thinking about those Greek statues. I had an urge to rub my hands across his broad chest, feel the warmth and texture of his skin, the contours of his muscles.

"I did eventually, but it seemed an eternity before he would let me. In the meantime he did things to my body— Well, other men had imitated what he did, but the way Edgar did them was authentic, all new and special. I felt treasured, as if the two of us were the only people in the world.

"He did eventually lie down on the bed beside me, and I soon realized, I understood at last, what he meant by making love.

"He whispered my name, used soft words, posed delicate questions, made gentle comments. He asked me if I was experiencing pleasure. No one had ever done that, not seriously. But he was sincere. When I moved beneath him, my body had a will of its own. The responses he stimulated in me were ordained, inevitable, instinctive. Every motion, every pulse and throb brought a demand for more.

"Even so, I was unprepared for what happened next, unprepared for the explosion that would shower me with sensations I'd never experienced as I reached my first orgasm.

"What had started as a moan rose to a scream I couldn't restrain. 'Oh,' I cried out. 'Oh.'

"He covered my mouth with his and sent me again into an oblivion filled with colors and skyrockets."

"Wow!" Sarah said.

"Yeah." Evvie grinned. "Wow!"

Chapter 11

" That afternoon of lovemaking changed everything," Edgar confessed. "In another time and
place I would have reached down, swung Evvie onto the
back of my white charger and ridden off into the sunset
with her arms wrapped tightly around my waist. Our
world wasn't nearly that ideal.

"Today, with the advantage of hindsight, we know
what was in store for us, but at the time all we could
be sure of was that the world at large was in chaos.

"Japan had attacked China and was inflicting terrible
suffering. In Europe other wars were raging. The
Spanish had fought a bloody civil war. The Italians had
marched into Abyssinia. The Germans were either

annexing their neighbors or attacking them. They were blitzing England and had invaded their ally Russia.

"Americans wanted no part in it. We remained aloof, focused on what was happening here at home. In spite of the Roosevelt administration's valiant efforts to enact social programs and put people to work, the nation's economy hadn't recovered. The private sector still wasn't hiring, and beyond life's basic necessities, people couldn't afford to buy much.

"Even Cousin Zeke was having a hard time. One of the things I'd learned that my parents didn't know was that Zeke had made his money as a bootlegger during Prohibition. Illegally imported whiskey and rum and domestically manufactured moonshine had given him the capital to purchase a big, fancy house in the Santa Rita district, along with several choice pieces of property in other parts of town.

"I discovered he was also a slumlord, renting out ramshackle houses to people who were desperate for a roof over their heads, even a leaky one. I'll say this for him…he didn't charge exorbitant rent for the dives—probably because he was shrewd enough to realize he couldn't get it—and I never heard of him actually evicting anyone who didn't pay, though he threatened to often enough. It was one of those little ironies that this cigar-chomping wise guy thought of himself as a kind of Robin Hood, a benevolent renegade with a heart of gold.

"Anyway, by the beginning of the forties, the lavish

lifestyle Zeke had grown accustomed to and that he took great glee in flaunting was becoming more difficult to maintain. He'd had the foresight to buy the car dealership with his ill-gotten loot right after Prohibition was repealed in '33. In spite of the obscene profits he was making on ancient Model T's and equally broken-down Model A's, however, he really wasn't doing all that well.

"He and his wife, Selma, had invited me to live with them rent free when my folks went off to Africa, and for a while I did. Their house was nice enough, but I soon realized it was constant bedlam. Selma was a raving alcoholic and apparently had been for years.

"They'd had a son back in the twenties. When the boy was five, she decided to take him to meet her family in Mississippi. That, at least, was one version of the story. Another was that she'd had enough of Zeke's womanizing and walked out on him. Whatever the reason, while they were there, the boy contracted yellow fever and died.

"Why she ever came back to San Angelo, I don't know and I never asked. Once back, though, she began hitting the bottle pretty heavy.

"What was the name of that movie years ago with Liz Taylor and Richard Burton? *Who's Afraid of Virginia Woolf.* Well, let me tell you, those movie characters had nothing on Zeke and Selma. They were constantly bickering, yelling obscenities that would have made a G.I. blush and throwing things. After Selma finally went to bed at night or as often passed out on the couch—once on the staircase—Zeke would have his buddies over for all-night card games that included more cusswords than they had aces up their sleeves. I've never been a saint, in spite of my parents' upright example, but even I couldn't take the hubbub for very long.

"I found myself a room for two dollars a week in a house about a ten-minute walk from Zeke's car dealership and another twenty minutes from downtown. It was a dinky little place, only marginally clean. No meals provided and no cooking allowed, but it was the best I could afford, and since I didn't do more than sleep there, it didn't much matter.

"I continued to work for Cousin Zeke. No salary, just commissions, but I was grateful for the job. I was a fairly competent salesman, but I wasn't making any money to speak of. People weren't buying cars, new or used, and I had expenses that were mounting.

"Besides paying room rent, I had to buy all my meals, and eating out all the time was expensive. I rarely ate more than two meals a day, sometimes only one. No all-you-can-eat-buffets in those days, and portions weren't big enough to warrant doggie bags. There were the usual living expenses: laundry, haircuts, razor blades. Nobody wore beards in those days. I darned my own socks. The clothes I'd brought from China were a couple of years old and were either too small now or threadbare, so I'd been forced to borrow money from Cousin Zeke for new duds, including shoes, and had to pay him back. More than anything, though, now that I'd made love with Evvie, I wanted to spend time alone with her, away from Miss Hattie's.

"Where?

"My boardinghouse was off limits. Zeke and Selma's was out of the question, and we couldn't go to her mother's place. The Cactus Hotel cost two-fifty a night. The Naylor, across the street from Miss Hattie's, was two bucks, and the places that were cheaper, well, they might be all right for other people's quickie sex, but not for making love.

"There was only one solution. I had to purchase my time with Evvie *at* Miss Hattie's. That cost two dollars, too, but Evvie always gave me back the dollar she got out of it when she turned in my token. Believe me, I wasn't happy with the arrangement and neither was she, but we were desperate for each other as only two young people can be. Remember, I was nineteen years old. She was only sixteen.

"Young and in love.

"I was also a man, and a man has his pride. The idea of having to pay for my time with Evvie was bad enough, but the thought that other guys were having sex with my girl tore me apart. So, before long we began fighting.

"I wanted her to leave Miss Hattie's. I begged her to.

"'How am I going to feed my family?' she'd snap back.

"'I'll help,' I'd say lamely.

"She'd laugh. 'Yeah, sure. How do you propose to do that? You can barely afford to pay your rooming-house rent.'

"That hurt.

"'You probably have to borrow the two bucks from Zeke to come here and see me,' she added.

"Now, *that* was hitting below the belt. It was doubly humiliating because it was also true.

"'Don't tell me you'll get another job. If there were other jobs available, you'd have one.' Then she'd soften. 'If I could do something else, honey, I would. If there was any other work out there, I'd take it. But I've looked. There isn't. Not for you and not for me. Not in San Angelo.'

"I did manage to pick up a few odd jobs from time to time, patching roofs, mowing lawns, shoveling manure, even cleaning outhouses. Slug work, but I didn't complain. I was grateful for whatever I could latch on to because it meant extra cash. Unfortunately there weren't enough of those jobs around and they didn't pay well, not nearly enough to equal what Evvie was making at Miss Hattie's.

"'We'll go somewhere else,' I said.

"It didn't take her long to shoot that idea down, either. Her brother had moved to California, the golden land, but he wasn't faring very well, and how would we get to wherever it was we were going? We didn't have a car or money to buy one, nothing to barter in a deal. Even if Cousin Zeke gave us one, aside from the fact that it would be a clunker that would no doubt leave us stranded in the middle of nowhere, how were we supposed to buy gasoline without money? What would we live on along the way? Also, Evvie absolutely refused to leave her mother and the children, and I couldn't in good conscience ask her to.

"We were stuck.

"Evvie would lay her head on my chest and cry. As much as I loved her at those times, I hated myself more.

"I had to do something. After all, I was a man. Earning a living was my responsibility.

"I kept job hunting. No Internet back then. I walked over to the library every day and checked newspaper want ads. There weren't many here or in other towns and cities. I wrote a few letters of inquiry, even went to the expense of making a couple of long-distance telephone calls. A waste of money.

"I was an American who'd spent most of his life outside the country and had few marketable skills. I could ride a horse, but I wasn't a cowboy. I could speak half a dozen languages, but Spanish wasn't one of them. I even considered preaching, but most of the heathens I'd met in San Angelo were already Christian, and there was no shortage of parsons willing to lead them back to the fold. After a while I actually felt grateful to Cousin Zeke for giving me any job at all.

"I didn't only want Evvie to leave Miss Hattie's—I wanted to marry her, to make her my wife, the mother of my children. That's what she wanted, too, but...

"If it had been only the two of us, we could have struck out on our own, hitchhiked to Dallas or another big city, where I could have found the kind of work I was capable of doing, as a teacher or a salesman. Surely she could have found something, sewing for a dressmaker or tailor or waiting on tables. She was willing to scrub floors, anything. As long as we could be to-gether...as long as she didn't have to turn tricks.

"She'd told me about the hours she'd spent trudging up and down every street in town, looking for sewing and darning jobs, asking people to let her wash dishes, clean house, garden, mind kids. Even when she did get other piddly jobs, they didn't pay enough to live on, and they didn't produce steady, dependable income. Miss Hattie did.

"We didn't know what we were going to do. I hated her taking other men into 'our' bed. I was worried about her physical safety, and I had reason to be."

Chapter 12

"Edgar taught me what physical intimacy could and should be. Special, even sacred. Having experienced those exquisite sensations with Edgar, I didn't want to share them with anyone else.

"And I didn't. I saved my orgasms for him.

"When he left, it was as though a door slammed shut, or a movie theater that had been alive with excitement a moment earlier suddenly went dark and silent.

"By autumn my life had settled into a predictable routine. In the morning, before Miss Hattie's opened, I'd leave by the back stairs. Edgar would be waiting for me in the alley and together we'd walk to my mother's house. I had told her that Edgar was a salesman who had shown up to sell Miss Hattie a new car, which of course was completely true. I also told her he was the son of a preacher who was spreading the word of God to the heathens in Africa, which was also true. I didn't tell her he was one of my clients at Miss Hattie's, and she didn't ask.

"I played the dutiful daughter during my two-hour morning visits at home, ironed and folded clothes, talked about the price of beans and rice or a special sale on salt pork or chicken necks at the butcher shop. I'd help snap beans or shuck peas or blanch fresh fruit for peeling if Mom had gotten a bargain on a bushel of it for canning. Edgar spent the time entertaining the kids, giving them rides on his back, playing hide-and-seek, shooting marbles in the dirt. They loved having him around and he plainly enjoyed being with them. He would keep them—as well as Mom and me—spell-bound with his tales of far-off places. I was never sure how much of his stories was true, how much was legend he'd learned about in those exotic places and how much he flat-out made up. The kids hated to see him leave, but he always promised to return.

"He'd walk me back to Miss Hattie's, then go off to sell used cars for his cousin. The most he ever sold was two in one week and earned forty dollars. Some weeks he sold none.

"Upstairs I'd change from street clothes into a more provocative outfit, sit in the parlor thumbing through *Reader's Digest*, play dominoes with Elmo in the card room or listen to Al Jolson on the Victrola in the dining room and wait for the next man to hand me a token.

All the time I was counting the days, the hours, the minutes, until Edgar would show up and I could become passionately alive again.

"Mom and I received letters from my brother every week without fail. They usually contained a few bucks, occasionally a money order for a little more. It all helped, because there were always unplanned-for expenses. A new washtub when the old one sprang a hole. A threadbare sheet that got torn in the wind and had to be replaced. A cord of wood for the fireplace when the nights started to get cold.

"I missed Henry terribly. Until Edgar came into my life, he'd been my best friend. In San Angelo, my only friend. I missed our long conversations, his upbeat sense of humor, the feeling of being safe when I was with him.

"I'd thought a few times about writing Henry about what I was doing and why, but I always put it off. Then I met Edgar and realized I didn't have to. He was my confidant now, my soul mate in a way my brother could never be.

"Still, I couldn't resist telling Henry about Edgar, sharing the joy I found in being with him. Not where I'd met him, of course, or the complete nature of our relationship, but the rest of what I recounted was true— that I'd been working for a woman in town when he showed up to sell her a new car, that we took one look at each other and, well, we just knew.

"Henry wrote back and teased me about puppy love, insisting I was much too young to get serious about a fella, especially one so much older than me. Three years, as if Edgar had one foot in the grave and the other on a banana peel. Under all the razzing, though, I could tell Henry was happy for me. Mom had apparently mentioned Edgar in one of her letters, as well, because Henry commented that she also seemed partial to him. She hadn't said anything to me, or that she thought he was a real looker, but it pleased me that she approved of him, even though she must have realized our relationship went beyond innocent friendship.

"Wait till you meet him," I wrote Henry. "You'll like him, too. I know you will."

"I'd ask Henry when he was coming home. He always replied that he hoped it would be soon, but then he'd talk about California, about what a really swell place it was. The weather was perfect, he said, and you could grow anything there. Maybe we ought to consider moving out. But of course that was impossible, at least for the present. We didn't have money for train fare, no place to live when we got there, no steady work, and Dad was still at the McKnight Sanitarium.

"Edgar managed to borrow one of his cousin's more reliable used cars on one of my days off, and he drove Mom, me and the kids up to visit Dad.

"He was no longer considered contagious, but he wasn't getting any better, and he was so weak he spent most of his time in bed. He couldn't care for himself anymore, and bringing him home—as much as we wanted to—was out of the question. Mom was already wearing herself out, doing the wash and taking care of the kids by herself. Benjy had recently contracted the chicken pox, which had added to her burden. She'd put his little sister in bed with him, hoping Joan would get it, too, and be done with it, but she hadn't.

"Having Dad home would only complicate matters. He'd need to use a bedpan, for example, and he could barely feed himself. He'd also find out about me, and that would just about kill him. Dad wasn't a particularly religious person, but he was a moral man. He would rather die than find out his daughter had become a prostitute.

"I talked to Dr. McKnight and his administrator. They agreed that in addition to Dad requiring constant attention, the chances were high that he'd become contagious again, which would mean putting the children at risk. Staying at the sanitarium was the best solution. I had been sending seven dollars a week, the dollar a day they'd requested. They asked now if it would be possible to send more. I calculated in my mind and offered to double it. Fourteen dollars a week. They were satisfied with that.

"When I told Mom, she was torn. She wanted Dad home so much, and she felt guilty because she couldn't nurse him the way she thought she should. As his wife she considered it her duty. Hadn't she vowed to love him in sickness and in health? We all recognized that if the situation had been reversed, Dad would have done the same for her without complaint. Adding to her sense of failure was awareness of where the money would come from, but she also had an obligation to the orphaned children of her late brother-in-law.

"I observed Edgar with my father that day. He was absolutely wonderful. The two men became instant friends, and for that I was both relieved and grateful.

"If I hadn't already been head over heels in love with Edgar, I would have fallen for him that day. All those years in the missionary field had taught him sympathy and kindness. When we were finally ready to leave and Dad had to go back to his room, Edgar pushed his wheelchair, picked him up in his arms and put him in his bed. He did it with such natural compassion that Dad never lost his dignity, never was made to feel less of a man for needing help.

"We had a flat tire on the way home. Mom and I stood on the side of the road with the children and watched Edgar change it. The summer had turned into autumn, but no one had told the weatherman. The sun was sweltering that day. The temperature must have been close to a hundred degrees.

"I remember clearly the sight of Edgar drenched in sweat as he struggled with lug nuts that seemed to have been welded on. His worn cotton shirt clung to his broad back, outlining his well-toned muscles, and as I gazed upon him going about his task with patience and determination, I felt such a desire to possess him that it nearly brought me to tears. I loved that man with every fiber of my being, so intensely it frightened me. My heart ached as I wondered what would become of us."

Chapter 13

"Since my reason for visiting Miss Hattie's was no longer to sell her a car, I started using the back door like every other john. Evvie's room was the second on the right. I usually greeted her in passing on my way to the office to purchase a token, but that day I stopped short.

"Evvie was sitting on her bed, leaning on pillows piled against the white iron bedstead, paging through a pulp magazine. Something was wrong. I started to ask her what it was, when she raised her head. She was sporting a shiner. Her right eye was completely black and blue. I tore open the screen door.

"'What happened?' I implored, hoping with all my heart she'd tell me it was the result of an innocent accident, tripping on her own feet or the edge of the carpet.

"'It's nothing,' she mumbled and shyly lowered her head again.

"'It doesn't look like nothing to me,' I snapped. She cringed at my sharp tone.

"I sat down on the edge of the mattress and cupped her chin. She flinched at my touch, though I was gentle. This was no innocent pratfall. It was a nightmare. She was hurt. Worse than a nightmare. She was the most precious thing in the world to me, and I'd failed to protect her.

"'Tell me who did this,' I shouted.

"She pulled back from me and I felt like a heel. The last thing I wanted was for her to be afraid of me. I loved her. Didn't she realize that? I would never do anything to harm her—or let anybody else hurt her.

"I was about to apologize and pull her into my arms, when Miss Hattie opened the screen door and walked in as though she owned the place. Well, she did, of course, but… My raised voice had undoubtedly brought her.

"'She's fine,' she said behind me.

"I put my back up, automatically shielding Evvie, as if Hattie were the enemy, and it occurred to me maybe she was. It wasn't unheard of for madams to be physically abusive to their girls, though I couldn't imagine this woman being so, or Evvie not telling me if she was.

"'Look at her. She's not fine. What happened?' I demanded. 'Who did this to her?'

"Evvie kept her head bowed. Hattie stepped deeper into the tiny room, closed the door and stood at the foot of the bed, facing me.

"'One of her callers got a little rambunctious this morning.'

"I felt sick.

"While I'd been sitting around the showroom, waiting for the next chump to venture onto the lot... While I was daydreaming about getting Evvie out of this place so I could have her all to myself, some bastard was treating her like a punching bag. Fury rose in me. I was disgusted with myself and deeply ashamed. What kind of man allowed the woman he loved to screw other men, to be used and abused by them?

"Evvie shuffled around so she could sit next to me. She took my hand, patiently pried open the fist I'd formed and fit her small palm against mine.

"My heart was pounding. 'Why?' I asked her, hardly able to breathe.

"'He...' She hesitated.

"'He had trouble performing,' Hattie explained for her. 'It happens sometimes, especially with older men. He blamed her for his lust and took it out on her when he wasn't able to follow through on it.'

"'He didn't have a problem the last time he was here,' Evvie mumbled, refusing to lift her head. Which was probably as well. Making eye contact with her now would only have reinforced the shame I felt for allowing her to be here. I didn't want to think of her naked with other men, touching them, letting them touch her.

"'He'd been here before?'

"'Several times,' Miss Hattie told me. 'Until today, he's never been violent.'

"Was she blaming Evvie for this Neanderthal's in-adequacy?

"I demanded to know his name. I planned to find the son of a bitch and introduce him to my version of the fear of God. My daddy firmly believed in turn-ing the other cheek. I did, too. After I'd beaten the crap out of him. I had no tolerance for cowards who struck women.

"'You don't have to worry about him coming around anymore,' Miss Hattie assured me. 'I've put out the word. The next time he wants a woman he'll have to do some traveling.'

"'What are you talking about?'

"Miss Hattie's bordello, I learned, was on a circuit of brothels that included Brownwood, Abilene, Lubbock, Midland and San Antonio. A few of the girls rotated among the six houses at regular intervals, variety being good for business. When a customer got out of hand—for unacceptable behavior, violence, excessive drunken-ness or disease—he was put on a blacklist and found himself banned from reputable 'gentlemen's clubs' in those cities. His only alternative then was to take his chances with streetwalkers in the shadier parts of town.

"After a few more minutes, I finally calmed down. Miss Hattie allowed me to stay that afternoon without charge, probably because her other clients wouldn't be turned on by damaged goods anyway. I expected to forgo sex that day, but Evvie said she needed to make love with me to remind her there was still beauty in the world. I was extra gentle that afternoon, but no less passionate.

"That didn't stop me afterward from begging her again to quit the place.

"'I hate this,' I argued, 'constantly thinking about what you're doing with other men.'

"She flared at me. 'Is that what this is all about? Your injured pride? You can't stand the thought that I'm bouncing the springs with someone besides you?'

"My blood boiled. I saw red. I was furious. I've never subscribed to the Latin code that allows a man to kill an unfaithful spouse or lover, but I understand the emotion. I wanted to strike out, put my fist through a wall, smash objects. Had there been a cord of wood nearby I could have pummeled it into matchsticks.

"I dragged in several long deep breaths to wrestle my anger under control. 'It's not just that,' I countered.

"'But that's part of it.'

"Exasperated, I glared at her. 'Of course that's part of it, Evvie. How can it not be? If the situation were reversed, how would you feel about me having sex with other women?'

"Her lower lip trembled. She faced the window.

"'Remember what I told you the first time, Evvie? Remember what I said? That I didn't want to have sex with you—I wanted to make love with you. I thought that was what we did. Made love. Or was I, am I, just another john?'

"She spun around. 'No! I didn't mean that. It's not the same with you.'

"'What you do with them and what you do with me

is,' I pointed out. 'It drives me crazy knowing you're making other men feel the way I do.'

"'I don't love them,' she replied angrily and even more hurt. 'I love you, damn it. That's the difference, Edgar. I love you.'

"A minute of silent gloom elapsed before I realize those words should never be spoken in anger. But they were that day. The most beautiful words in any language and we were using them as a weapon?

"'I love you, too,' I responded more gently. 'That's why you have to give up this life.'

"'Give up?' she flared anew. 'You make it sound as if I like *this life*. Have you forgotten why I'm here, Edgar? Why I became a hooker? To feed hungry children, Edgar. To keep a roof over their heads. To put clothes on their backs and buy them medicine. Give up this life? You're asking me to give up *their* lives.'

"I understood all that, and she knew it. Yet she was making me sound selfish because I didn't want her earning a living in a bordello.

"'Evvie, what you're doing is dangerous. The man who attacked you today may not have seriously hurt you, but what about the next creep who can't get it up and decides to punish you for it? He could do serious, permanent damage.'

"She started to say something, but I cut her off. 'Don't tell me it won't happen, Evvie. It happened once. It can happen again, and we both know it.'

"She turned her back on me. 'Please go, Edgar. Leave me alone.'

"I ignored her entreaty and spoke to her hunched shoulders. 'What about disease? What happens if you get the clap?'

"The only protection against venereal disease back then was condoms, but you could only purchase them in drugstores, where they were kept under the counter, out of sight. You had to nod the pharmacist over to the side and whisper in his ear what you wanted. Most men weren't willing to go through that indignity. Rubbers, as we called them, were also expensive, too expensive for the girls to furnish, even if they could convince their customers to use them.

"And of course there was the threat of pregnancy. Miss Mable had a baby. I had to wonder if I could be as magnanimous as her sick husband about a child who wasn't mine. I liked to think I would be, but that old male ego kept bugging me, making me question whether I wouldn't always look at the kid and be reminded that another man had planted the seed.

"I didn't raise that subject, though. For one thing, I was sure Evvie had thought about it herself. For another, I could tell by the way her shoulders were trembling that she was crying. I had made her cry. The woman I loved, and I was making her cry. A new fist of shame gut punched me, making me feel queasy.

"Cautiously I reached for her, intending to turn her around and hold her in my arms, but when she felt my touch, she pulled stiffly away, straightened her spine, heaved a huge breath, let it out slowly, spun around to confront me.

"'Okay, wise guy, since you seem to have all the answers, what am I supposed to do when I leave here? Go home, dear Edgar, and watch my mother work herself to death while the kids get sick and die of malnutrition? Am I going to regain my virtue by sacrificing them on the altar of your pride? You're a big strong fellow, and you can't even earn enough money to get laid without going into debt to your cousin.'

"She was on a roll. 'There's something you better understand, Edgar. I'm a floozy, a harlot. I earn a living turning tricks, letting men screw me. You were fully aware of that when you met me. Nothing has changed, big man. I'm still a whore.'

"'Stop,' I shouted and squeezed my eyes shut. 'Stop,' I moaned.

"I moved up to her and put my arms around her. She resisted for a moment, but it didn't last. I folded her in a tender embrace. 'Stop, Evvie. Please, don't say those things.'

"She rested her head against my chest, wetting my shirt with her tears. I could feel her whole body sobbing. 'Not saying them doesn't change anything, Edgar.'

"'We'll find a way.'

"'Well, when you do, be sure to let me know. Until then, this is who I am, what I do.'

"I tilted her head up. Her eyes were glassy, bruised. 'What you do maybe, but not who you are.'

"After that episode we fought regularly. We'd make love, then fight. Sometimes we'd end up making love again, but as often as not I left Miss Hattie's angry."

★ ★ ★

"I was losing him. He inevitably arrived with a warm smile and a gentle touch. I felt so at home in his arms, but our lovemaking, while always good, was becoming more desperate on his part, as if he was trying to compete, to prove to me that he was better than the others.

"I wanted to tell him he had nothing to worry about, that he had no rivals, no competition, but I was afraid to say even that, as though by doing so I would be acknowledging that there were others.

"As often as not, when he left he was angry. He tried not to show it, but it was becoming more and more difficult for him to hide it. I understood what he was feeling. I also realized it was only a matter of time before the heat of his anger overwhelmed the warmth of our pleasure, and he would be gone. Then I would be completely alone.

"That night, every night, I cried myself to sleep."

Chapter 14

"The bombing of Pearl Harbor was a shock to everyone," Edgar said, "but I can't say I was totally surprised by it. I had no special insight that the Japanese were going to hit Hawaii specifically, but having lived a good part of my life in the Orient, it seemed inevitable to me that our two nations would soon be at war. In China I'd witnessed what the Imperial Japanese juggernaut was capable of doing, and it wasn't pretty.

"That Sunday night, December 7, I visited Evvie and told her I was going to volunteer for military service.

"'We haven't even declared war yet,' she objected.

"'We will. We have to. American territory has been bombed. Most of our fleet sunk. Thousands of people, military and civilian, have been killed. We can't ignore it. We can't pretend it didn't happen. Believe me, the Japs won't stop with Pearl Harbor. This is just the beginning.'

"She gave me a dirty look. 'Convenient, isn't it, Edgar?'

"I gaped at her. 'Convenient? What are you talking about?'

"'You hate what I do, what I am, but you can't do anything about it, so you're running away.'

"I was dumbfounded. The world was at war, our national survival was on the line, and she was thinking only about herself.

"'You're damn right I hate what you're doing.' I kept my voice down, but that didn't diminish the emotion in it. 'Do you have any idea what it's like for me to know you're spreading your legs for every guy who comes in here and plops down a token? Do you, Evvie?'

"She pulled back, her cheeks turned red, her beautiful green eyes glassy. I was hurting her and that made me more furious at both of us. 'I'm a man up here, too, Evvie,' I cried as I jammed my index fingers against my temples. 'I'm a man, Goddamnit.'

"I spun away from her, unwilling to let her see my frustration and shame. After a minute, I faced her again.

"'Our country has been attacked. I can't save you from the life you've chosen—'

"'I've chosen?' she sputtered in outrage.

"'But I can help defend my country. You don't know what the Japanese war machine is like. I do. I can't stand by and let it happen here. If we don't fight them now in the Pacific, in China, on their turf, we'll have to fight them later, here, on ours. They won't stop with Hawaii, Evvie. Next will be San Francisco and Seattle.'

"'They can't occupy the whole country,' she argued. 'We're too big.'

"'You don't think so? Well, you're wrong. China is big, too, and they have a lot more people than we do, but the Japanese took it over anyway. They occupy it and control it. Don't you understand? It's now or later, but one way or another, we'll have to fight them.'

"She sighed. 'You're right, of course, and I'm proud of you for wanting to fight for our country, but—'

"'But what?'

"She put her arms around me. 'I'm scared, Edgar. Scared of losing you.'

"'Nothing's going to happen to me.'

"'Tell that to the boys in Flanders Field.'

"I paused a moment, recollecting the mournful poem written by a Canadian army doctor commemorating the dead of the Great War.

"'You'll be all right.' I held her, felt the warmth of her body igniting mine. 'That's why we've got to fight. To make sure you and your mom and the kids, and everybody else's kids, are safe.'

"'I don't want you to go.' I heard panic in her voice.

"How could I tell her that I did? Not to get away from her, but because nothing would ever change if I stayed.

"I would go insane if I had to continue standing around Cousin Zeke's dealership, waiting to fleece the next poor sucker who walked in, then take my ill-gotten gains to Miss Hattie's so I could lie, one man among many, with the woman I loved. The rage in me was building. I needed to get control of my life, channel my energy, feel my muscles grow and harden, not atrophy under a shirt and tie.

"'I have to go, sweetheart.' I gazed down at her. 'Don't you understand? I have to be a man.'

"'Why can't you wait until you're called?'

"She was bargaining for every minute we could have together. I ached those minutes, as well. I loved her body and soul, but at that stage in my life being with her wasn't enough. Not in those circumstances. I craved to be part of something bigger, something decisive. Like most of the boys I'd talked to, I was spoiling for a fight. Drought and depression had built up our tempers. We were tired of shadowboxing with forces we couldn't see, couldn't touch, couldn't ram our fists into.

"I understood Evvie's point, too. We'd been lovers for nearly six months, during which we'd explored sensations and impulses that had made us feel more alive than we ever had. Lately, though, our mutual pleasure hadn't been enough. We seemed to spend more time fighting than delighting each other. Oh, the sex was still great, but with each passing interval physical gratification felt counterfeit if I couldn't have her exclusively.

"The next morning, I appeared at the recruiting station along with a lot of other Joes eager to even the score, and signed up for the duration."

"What would you have done if the war hadn't

broken out, Gramps, and you couldn't have gotten Grandma to leave Miss Hattie's?"

Edgar paused, gazed off into space for a minute, before replying without pride, "I would have had to leave, son, just like her brother did, to find work elsewhere. I would have told her how much she meant to me, how much I loved her, wanted to be with her always, and I would have promised to come back for her as soon as I could afford to support her. Then I would have left her."

"The news that the Japanese had attacked Pearl Harbor came as a complete shock to me," Evvie admitted. "Oh, like the other girls at Miss Hattie's, I was aware there was a war going on over in Europe, the English were fighting the Germans and the Germans were fighting the Russians, but I really hadn't paid much attention to any of it. What took place a million miles away didn't seem very important. Heck, I wasn't seventeen years old yet. I should have been in high school, worrying about grades, about whether the dreamboat in my class was going to ask me to the next dance, about the dress I was going to wear if he did. Why should I give a hang about world affairs?

"But everything changed on December 7, 1941, and for the next four years what went on a million miles away became very, very important to everybody.

"Edgar visited me that Sunday night. He didn't get a token from Miss Hattie, and for once she didn't seem interested in selling him one. All any of us had done that day was crowd around the Philco in the dining room and talk about the Japanese, about whether they would strike us here in the States and how we were going to beat them.

"I suppose I realized even before Edgar said anything that he was going to enlist. The thought scared me so much I flew into a rage and accused him of signing up to get away from me.

"I was being stupid and selfish, but all I could think of was what would happen to me if he got killed. He tried to assure me nothing bad would happen to him, and I clearly was not convinced, which didn't help matters.

"We fought that evening. Instead of making love, we fought."

Edgar curled his fingers around his coffee mug. "I was still so hot under the collar about the things Evvie had said—fuming because she'd been at least partially right: I was running away. I didn't go to be with her Monday night. Instead I did something I'd never done. I got stinking drunk.

"My parents didn't use alcohol, and my single clandestine experiment with it when I was about fourteen convinced me I could do without the stuff, as well, but that Monday night I went over to Cousin Zeke's and tied one on. I drank whatever he or Selma handed me and, I'm told, passed out long before midnight, muttering unkind things about Evvie while protesting how much I loved her. Calling myself a low-down piece of crap for letting other guys screw my girl, at the same time I begged her to take me back because I couldn't live without her."

★ ★ ★

"He stayed away Monday night," Evvie continued, "which only proved to me he didn't really love me. I told myself as far as he was concerned I'd been nothing more than a cheap piece of ass he didn't need anymore. He'd go away and find some other girl to screw.

"Then I'd stop and my heart would ache. Suppose I never saw him again. Suppose he went off to fight and never came back."

"You can imagine what I felt like Tuesday morning," Edgar said with a chuckle, "or rather Tuesday afternoon, since I slept until twelve-thirty. I was able to work up the courage to eat a sandwich around three o'clock, and by five I was beginning to entertain the notion that I might live. I vowed never to let demon rum touch my lips again. It wasn't worth the suffering.

"By eight o'clock that evening all the aspirin I'd taken had finally done its job and I was actually feeling human again. Human, male and passionate."

"Tuesday night, our last night together, he showed up—" Evvie sighed "—and immediately I could tell there was something different about him. He wasn't wearing a uniform yet, but he might as well have been. He carried himself with the masculine pride and confidence of a warrior in shining armor. He'd always excited me, but that night I felt overwhelmed by him. Overwhelmed, a little afraid and aroused in a way I'd never experienced. We couldn't get enough of each other.

"He'd told me he loved me many times in the past, but now those words took on a frantic quality. He kept repeating them and promising he would always love me. If he didn't survive the war, he said, he wanted me to know I was the most wonderful thing that had ever happened to him. We closed the door and he stayed the night, all night. Being December, I had a little coal stove set up to heat the room, but in our passion for each other we forgot about it and the fire went out. The room grew cold. The only way for me to keep warm was to cling to Edgar, and I did. Desperately. In some ways it was the most perfect time we'd ever spent together."

"If Edgar hadn't gone off to war and he'd made leaving Miss Hattie's a condition of his love, what would you have done?" Sarah asked.

"I'm not sure exactly, but I would have found a way. Somehow, I would have found a way."

"Our last night together was unlike any I'd ever spent with Evvie," the old man said, "knowing I was going away and wouldn't see her for a long time…that I might never come back…or in what condition…that kind of uncertainty raises passion above the physical to a plane that's…spiritual. The memory of our lovemaking, I can tell you, sustained me through a lot of what followed. I worried about her. I prayed for her as I marched off to war.

"I was twenty years old. Big, strong and immortal."

Chapter 15

"About a week into basic training," Edgar continued, "I was yanked out of maneuvers and interviewed by a board of officers. I'd put down on my enlistment application that I was an experienced aviation pilot, having learned to fly in China where I routinely transported my perpetually airsick father to missions in different parts of the country. They grilled me about my flying skills, then offered me a commission as an officer in the air corps. I could hardly turn that down.

"I transferred from Brownwood, Texas, to Reno Army Air Field in Nevada for flight training. I was hoping the troop train would go through San Angelo and I'd be able to meet Evvie, if only for a few minutes, but it went north through Abilene and Lubbock, so I didn't even get to wave to her from the window. I'd gotten only one letter off to her, written under the blanket with the help of a flashlight late at night, telling her how much I missed her. There hadn't been time to receive an answer from her.

"At Reno we trained six, sometimes six and a half days a week. For me it was more about learning military procedures, tactics and airframes than the art of flying. Long days, mentally and physically, starting before sunrise and lasting well past dark. I grumbled like everybody else, but I loved being so active. The food may not have been great, but there was plenty of it, and the weight I gained was in hard muscle.

"During our short breaks we pored over newspapers and listened to the radio for any information about what was going on overseas.

"Germany and Italy had declared war on us four days after Pearl Harbor. In the Pacific, MacArthur pulled out of the Philippines with his staff, abandoning a large contingent of beleaguered troops, female nurses, dependents and civilians to fend for themselves, which would soon result in the Bataan Death March.

"In April of '42 Jimmy Doolittle raised everybody's morale by bombing Tokyo just to let the emperor know we weren't licked.

"Evvie and I continued to exchange letters. I savored every word. She told me about her mother, her brother, the children, what was going on in town, war drives. She talked about everything except Miss Hattie's. I was grateful. I didn't want to be reminded of how she spent her afternoons and evenings. Still, I couldn't stop thinking about her being there and why. I started a few times to beg her to leave the place, but I knew it wouldn't do any good. She would leave when she could, and I didn't dare make her mad at me, for fear she'd stop writing. What I did tell her was how much I loved her and longed to be with her again."

"The day after Edgar reported for induction, my mother received a letter from my brother. Henry, too, had signed up. Mom was in tears.

"As I tried to console her, I kept thinking how wonderful it would be if he and Edgar were assigned to the same outfit and could serve together. It didn't happen. As soon as the army realized Edgar already knew how to fly, they transferred him to pilot training. Henry had finished high school, but he had no special skills. He was assigned to the infantry, one of millions of privates toting rifles. He did his basic training at Fort Ord, but we weren't ready to fight ground battles in the Pacific theater of operations yet, so the army sent him clear across the country to Fort Bragg in Georgia for advanced weapons training.

"On his way east he was able to finagle a three-day pass to visit us. The best part was that he'd be here for my seventeenth birthday. I was ecstatic and scared at the same time. Suppose he found out about Miss Hattie's.

"He arrived the night before my birthday and had to leave early the morning after it. Since we had only one full day together, the first in over a year, I was determined we would have it as a family, which meant going up to Carlsbad to visit Dad. There weren't any rental-car agencies in those days, so I went to Edgar's cousin Zeke to beg him to lend us a car for the day. I was willing to pay whatever he asked. I even wondered if he might suggest taking it out in trade, since he was aware of me working at Miss Hattie's. To my surprise he didn't want any money and he didn't so much as hint at me paying him with favors. Perhaps the idea of doing his cousin's girl was too much even for him. Or he might have been afraid of what would happen if Edgar ever found out. Most likely he just thought furnishing transportation so my brother could see our dad was the right thing to do.

"Regardless of the reason, I was very grateful when he told me to bring Henry around and he'd let us have whatever was available on the used-car lot. I expected a tin lizzie, but we received a nearly new top-of-the-line DeSoto sedan. Edgar had told me his cousin could be a real charmer when he was in the mood. Well, that day he was the soul of discretion and an absolute gentleman.

"Mom and I were both surprised at how good Henry looked. He'd always been slender, and he still was, but now he seemed lean and fit rather than skinny. All those months of working outdoors had given him a golden tan. A real poster boy was my brother, so handsome in his uniform.

"I'd been worried Henry would start asking me questions about my work and how much I was getting paid for it. I needn't have. On the trip up to Carlsbad, Mom rambled on about how much I helped her with the laundry and minding the kids, and that I sewed for people whenever I got a chance, which, after I thought about it, was true. The girls at Miss Hattie's did still occasionally bring me things that needed mending, though they didn't offer to pay me for the work anymore. So the tense moments I'd feared never developed.

"Dad was, of course, overjoyed to see his son. He cried, and that made the rest of us cry, too.

"Mom had fixed a picnic hamper, and the day was warm enough for us to sit at one of the outdoor tables. We gorged ourselves on fried chicken, potato salad and corn pone. Then Mom brought out the pecan pie she'd baked with the pecans she'd somehow found time to gather herself down along the river. Pecan pie was my favorite and she always made me one for my birthday. She put eighteen little candles in it, seventeen for my age and one to grow. I smiled and got misty-eyed when everybody sang "Happy Birthday" to me, and I bit my lips when they presented me with their gifts.

"My brother was the first. He brought me a slab of white quartz about the size of a half dollar with a splendid showing of gold winding through it, a souvenir of the Golden State. Clearly he'd fallen in love with California. I hugged him tight and promised to keep it always, and I have.

"Mom gave me what she'd brought. The silver-and-ivory vanity set, hairbrush, comb and hand mirror that had been her grandmother's. I threw my arms around her and broke down in tears, raising my father's and brother's eyebrows at my overreaction. They didn't recognize the significance of the gift.

"Mom eased me away, looked me in the eye and said everything was all right. I understood then that she'd forgiven me for my terrible decision.

"Oh, the pie was rich and sweet. I ate two big pieces.

"Late that afternoon we dropped Mom and the kids off at the house and I went with my brother to return the car.

"'Dad's not improving,' he said as we waited for the old man at the gas station on Beauregard to finish filling the tank and checking the water and oil. 'He's worse than when I left.'

"'He doesn't seem to be getting better,' I admitted.

"Henry paid the attendant and we got under way again. 'I have a terrible feeling, sis, that this is the last time I'll ever see him. I wish all these months I could have been here for him, for you and Mom, but I didn't know what else to do.'

"Would he understand if I told him what I had done under the circumstances?

"'You did the right thing, Henry. We're all very proud of you.'

"I yearned with all my heart for him to be proud of me. Maybe he would understand and forgive me for the choice I'd made, but I couldn't take the chance he might recoil from me the way Mom had. Losing my big brother, too, would be more than I could bear.

"We dropped off the car. Zeke shook Henry's hand, wished him good luck and told him to take care of himself.

"'Now, tell me about this used-car salesman you're so head over heels about,' Henry said as we started the mile-long walk back to the house.

"He was teasing me, but I refused to be rattled. I raved on about Edgar, about how big and strong and handsome he was. How smart. That he'd traveled all over the world and spoke a bunch of foreign languages and knew how to fly a plane even before he went into the army, so they were going to make him an officer.

"Henry laughed. 'An officer, huh? I figured he was too good to be true.'

"I took umbrage. 'Ask Mom if you don't believe me.'

"He squeezed my hand. 'I did, and she seems to agree with you. I'm jealous of this fella who's stolen both your hearts away from me.'

"I stopped, raised myself on tiptoe and pecked him on the cheek. 'That'll never happen.'

"'Nevertheless I'm looking forward to meeting this paragon of virtue.'

"'You'll love him, too,' I said.

"He put his arm around me and gave me a big hug. 'I'm glad to see you so happy, sis. I hope you will always be.'

"The next morning Henry got on a train heading east, and I was miserable. That night I sat down and wrote Edgar a long letter, pouring out my unhappiness, but I couldn't send it, so I tore it up and wrote a second version that was more upbeat. I told him all about Henry's visit, about how generous his cousin Zeke had been, that Dad sent his regards and about how much I missed him."

"The high point of every day was mail call," Edgar told his grandson. "Evvie wrote me several times a week. She told me her brother had given her the best birthday present possible by coming home to visit on his way to fight in Europe, and thanks to dear Cousin Zeke, they'd all gotten up to Carlsbad to spend the day with her dad. She rambled on about how prices were rising on everything and how rationing, which was just beginning to be implemented, was making matters worse. As usual she never mentioned Miss Hattie's. Not once. Anyone finding one of her letters would have thought she was the ideal girl next door. But she didn't say she'd left Miss Hattie's, either."

Chapter 16

"I spent forty-five cents on an oversize belated-birthday card for Evvie—most cards cost a dime—and double postage—six cents instead of three—and vowed never to forget her birthday again.

"I didn't write Evvie nearly as much as I should have or wanted to. Some of the guys wrote home nearly every day, especially if they had girls waiting for them. Lord knows what they talked about, except maybe to bitch about the canteen running out of Tootsie Rolls or Chiclets in the hope, I figured, that the folks back home would feel sorry for them and send goody packages. The ploy usually succeeded.

"I didn't really care about those things. Besides, I knew the source of the money for anything Evvie sent me. I did receive a batch of cookies from her mother. Mostly crumbs after bouncing around the postal system for two weeks, but I didn't care, and neither did the guys in the barracks I shared them with.

"Yet, as angry as I got when I thought about where Evvie was working and what she was doing, and as much as I missed her—and the sex we'd had—I didn't look for anyone to replace her. When we got rare time off, I hitched a ride into town with the rest of the boys but, staying true to my vow of abstinence, confined myself to Coke or lemonade at the dance halls we went to. Got some good-natured ribbing about it initially, too. What they didn't realize was that I didn't dare chance losing my inhibitions and wandering off with some gal. As much as I hated what Evvie did, I couldn't bring myself to be unfaithful to her.

"I have no idea what I talked about in my letters. They must have been boring. I tried paraphrasing a few Chinese love poems I'd learned, because they expressed my feelings far better than I ever could. They probably came across as trite, amateurish and sentimental. But there were things I didn't want to worry her about.

"Like our training losses. About twenty percent of the boys washed out for academic or physical reasons. Another twenty percent to accidents. I'm not talking about a broken arm or leg. Those healed and the casualty later returned to duty, though not necessarily to the flying program. I'm referring to injuries bad enough to send a guy home with a permanent disability or in a pine box.

"Like Johnny Court. He was my bunkmate, an easy-going fella from Tennessee whose birthday was three days after mine. We'd completed ground training and were in our third week of cockpit training when he and his instructor crashed short of the runway and were both killed.

"I'd witnessed death before. In the mission hospitals my father supported. I'd watched people die, so death wasn't as much of a stranger to me as it was to the boys in the outfit who'd never lost anyone close to them, but I have to admit Johnny's death got to me. He hadn't been sick. He wasn't old. He was a twenty-year-old like me in the best of health with his whole life ahead of him. Then suddenly he was gone. Forever. For the first time in my life I began to question my own mortality."

Evvie sipped her liquor. "On Friday, July 10, 1942, Mom received a letter from Dr. McKnight in the morning post saying Dad had passed away the afternoon before.

"Mom cried and so did I. I'd arranged, thanks again to Edgar's cousin Zeke, to hire a car and driver to take us up to Carlsbad the previous Sunday. We knew the end wasn't far off. Dad had grown increasingly feeble in the months after Henry's visit. Almost as if he'd given up, accepted he wasn't getting better, and it was time to let go. Neither of us would say it, even to ourselves, but his passing was a relief—for him and for us.

"The church ladies brought food to the house and

offered condolences, though most of them had never met my father and didn't really know my mother all that well. I'd stopped going to church months earlier. If they'd heard any rumors about me, they were discreet enough not to say anything. Zeke and his wife dropped by, which really surprised me. Miss Mable showed up with her young son, and Miss Rosie, who'd become my closest friend at Miss Hattie's, even brought food the girls had chipped in to buy from the restaurant that did our catering. Instead of her trademark red dress that day, Rosie wore a very plain dark burgundy outfit that was the epitome of modesty itself. I introduced them by name and left it at that. My mother wasn't stupid. She must have realized where I knew them from, but she never said a word and didn't ask any questions. Rosie also delivered a beautiful bouquet of flowers from a 'friend.' Reading the note, I recognized Miss Hattie's handwriting.

"We buried Dad beside Uncle John and Aunt Louise. Life went on. Dad had been a constant, reassuring presence when I was growing up in Oklahoma, but since we'd moved to Texas, he had faded from our daily lives. Other than helping Mom dispose of his old clothes—most of them were so threadbare they ended up being given to the rag man—his passing didn't change my routine, and in a way that was the saddest part of all. It didn't seem right that a person who had been such a vital part of my life a few years earlier should disappear without leaving more than a ripple. Years went by before I realized he'd left much more than that, but at the time all I felt was emptiness and desolation.

"I wrote Edgar about Dad's passing, and he answered with a very sweet letter of condolence, telling me how much he'd enjoyed meeting him and how lucky I was to have two such good and loving parents. I wasn't quite sure if he was suggesting I'd disgraced them—I later realized he hadn't—but my emotions were so close to the surface at that point that every word, no matter how kindly intended, sounded like an indictment for what I had become.

"I have to add that Edgar wrote the most beautiful letters. They were like poetry. I loved reading and re-reading them and wished I could use words the way he did. Simple words, not flowery, but the combinations were like individual bouquets. So exquisite and rich. I've saved them all, of course."

"So where did they send you after you completed flight training?" Bram asked.

"China. And let me tell you, son, I was excited at the prospect."

Edgar lifted his mug to take a mouthful of the coffee, realized it was cold and set it down again.

"The American-supplied war effort against the Japanese in China wasn't going well. Claire Chennault's Flying Tigers were doing a hell of a job staving off Japanese attacks against Chiang Kai-shek's beleaguered Nationalists at Kunming, but the only way to get supplies to them was from British-controlled India, which meant crossing the Himalayas, the highest mountain range in the world.

"By May of '42, the ground situation had deteriorated so badly that General Stilwell was ordered out of Burma to the safety of India. Unlike MacArthur, Vinegar Joe didn't abandon his troops. He walked out with them. He was a crusty old cuss, as his nickname implies, and his men weren't exactly fond of him, but no one ever doubted where they stood with him, including the generalissimo himself, and no one ever questioned his personal courage. Eventually the Ledo Road would be built through the mountains and jungles linking India and China, but it would take most of the war years to complete and cost thousands of lives in the process. Stilwell objected when it was renamed after him, claiming the honor should go to the people who built it.

"In the meantime flights of C-47 Dakota and C-46 Commando transports were given the Herculean mission of carrying supplies to China over the hump. A lot of planes and crews didn't survive the treacherous trip. The collection of wrecked aircraft on the mountainsides along the route came to be known as the aluminum highway."

"That's what you were assigned to do?"

The old man nodded. "Yep."

"With your familiarity of the Far East and knowledge of Japanese and Chinese, I'm surprised the army didn't assign you to military intelligence."

Edgar chuckled. "Some people will tell you that's an

oxymoron, son. As I said, I'd mentioned my language skills to the recruiter when I signed up and again to the board of officers who interviewed me in basic training, but all they seemed interested in was my experience in the cockpit. That was fine with me. I really wasn't interested in interrogating prisoners or sitting at a desk, poring over papers and reports. I wanted to taste action, real action. I wanted to fly."

He looked around for the waitress to get a refill of coffee, but she was nowhere in sight. "Of course, getting to China proved to be a challenge in itself."

"You got to see Grandma before you left, I hope."

"I wanted to, believe me, but the army only operated in two modes. Hurry up and wait, and wait and hurry up. I'd received no immediate response to my volunteer request to join the Tigers back in May, then toward the end of July they decided they needed me there yesterday.

"It was usual to receive anywhere from a few days to a couple of weeks furlough before deploying overseas. I figured I would, too, and was really counting on it because I'd bought an engagement ring, and I wanted to go to San Angelo and ask Evvie to marry me.

"'Sorry, no furlough authorized,' I was told. They needed me so badly in China, I had to ship out immediately.

"'At least let me stop off at Goodfellow Field,' I begged.

"No dice. I was ordered to fly directly to San Antonio, pick up extra crew members and supplies, refuel and proceed on. Posthaste. There wasn't even time for me to write Evvie and ask her to take the train down to San Antone and meet me there.

"As it turned out, my layover was only for about an hour, barely enough to refuel and load the extra cargo. After supervising all that and meeting the additional crew members, I managed to break away and find a pay phone.

"I called the long-distance operator—no direct dial in those days—and gave her the number for Miss Hattie's in San Angelo. Busy. Miss Hattie had only one telephone and it was on her desk. I tried again a few minutes later. Still busy. I paced. I swore. I sweated, and I damn near cried. I finally got through on my third attempt.

"Clutching the engagement ring in my hand—the diamond wasn't much bigger than a chip—I quickly identified myself, told Miss Hattie I was calling long-distance and asked to speak to Evvie. There was the briefest pause. She said she'd have to check if Evvie was available and cupped her hand over the mouth. But not well enough. I heard her ask if Evvie was still busy with Spud, and I heard the other person—I think it was Rosie—tell her a few seconds later that they were still going at it hot and heavy.

"My heart sank at the same time my blood boiled. The image was so vivid I imagined I could hear the bedsprings squeaking from all the way down the hall. I was calling to tell the woman I loved I wanted to marry her, and she was screwing a john in our bed.

"Diplomatically Miss Hattie informed me that Evvie had just stepped out to buy the girls Cokes but she would be back in a few minutes. Since I was calling long-distance, she asked for my number so Evvie could call me back.

"I was nearly blind with rage. I told her I was at a pay phone and I didn't know what the number was, which was true. The little round medallion was missing from the middle of the dial.

"'If you could just wait a minute or two for her to return—' Miss Hattie said. But my copilot was signaling me that we were ready to take off. We were flying east, away from the sun and didn't want to lose daylight if we could avoid it.

"The picture swimming in my mind was driving me crazy. 'I have to go,' I said, and hung up.

"I stewed over that phone call for weeks, cursed Evvie and threw the ring away twice, but of course I went back each time and retrieved it.

"From there we flew on to southern Florida, then took off the next morning for Venezuela, where we rested for two days. See what I mean about hurry up and wait? Why the hell couldn't the rest stop have been in San Antonio or, better still, in San Angelo? We crossed the Atlantic to South Africa, which, at the time, was under British control. No satellite-tracking systems in those days. For long stretches we couldn't even make radio contact because we were in what they call skip zones, where signals didn't reach. If we'd had to ditch, our chances of being found were close to zero. I'd never gaze into Evvie's eyes again, never hold her in my arms, taste her kisses, make love with her, but those thoughts were too painful for me to contemplate. Anger was easier to deal with, and I had plenty of it as I pictured her down the hall with some guy who'd paid for the privilege of using her."

"Did you at least get to visit with your folks while you were in Africa?" Bram asked.

Edgar shook his head. "I would have liked to, since I hadn't seen them in over a year, but I didn't have enough time to arrange for that, either. My folks were in the Belgian Congo, more than fifteen hundred miles north of Cape Town. There was no scheduled air service between the two. Train lines weren't directly connected, and road travel was excruciatingly slow and very dangerous. Still, we might have arranged something if there had been time."

"So you went on to India?"

Edgar smiled. "And began a whole new part of my life."

Chapter 17

"In August of '42 Edgar deployed overseas. Of course, I wasn't aware of that until after the fact," Evvie pointed out. "What I did know was that he'd tried to telephone me from San Antonio. At the time I was...I was with a client and Miss Hattie hadn't bothered to interrupt. I was furious with her when I found out. That was the only occasion I ever raised my voice to her, I was so angry. I said things...well, let's just say my language was colorful. I stayed away for three days. Stayed away and cried. I would have given anything to talk to Edgar, to hear his voice, to hear him say he still loved me. I moped around my mother's house, pitched in with the washing and ironing, but in the end I went back to

Concho Avenue. Neither Miss Hattie nor I said a word about the incident or my absence, then or later.

"I didn't hear from Edgar for a whole month, and that scared the daylights out of me. Where was he? Was he safe? Was he thinking about me? Had he not written because he was mad at me? Because his letters had gotten lost? Or had he been killed and I just hadn't been told yet?

"When I finally did receive a letter from him, it was written on onionskin paper, which meant he was overseas. From the West Coast postmark I concluded he was somewhere in the Pacific theater. He didn't tell me where, only that he was doing a lot of flying. He also avoided mentioning his telephone call.

"But I didn't. I poured out my heart about how disappointed I was to have missed it. Miss Hattie had told me the excuse she'd used to cover for my not being able to come to the phone—that I was out buying Cokes—and I was tempted to repeat it, but I didn't want to lie to Edgar. I didn't want to tell him the truth, either, so I just left out that part, emphasizing instead how much I missed him and how much I longed to hear his voice again and be with him.

"After that, his letters became erratic. I might not get one for weeks, then there'd be three of them at once. I could tell, too, he wasn't receiving all of mine, because he would ask questions about things I'd already told him about. It was confusing and disconcerting."

"I spent three days in India," the old man went on, "resting, getting briefed on flying over the hump, talk-

ing to guys who'd already done it, a few of them repeatedly. At last it was my turn in the barrel. I climbed
into my Gooney Bird, which was what we called the
C-47, and lifted off with a cargo of fuel and arms for
Kunming. I was lucky. We didn't run into any adverse
weather, but there were still a couple of places where
I swear we topped mountain ridgelines by no more
than a few feet. Would we make it over the next peak?
Would the controls freeze up? Would we run out of gas
or stall out because of the altitude? We all let out a col-
lective breath on the downhill side of a range, only to
hold it again when we approached the next one. We
fought headwinds that battered and tossed us and
seemed to bring us to a dead stop. There were spots
when we swore we could have gotten out and walked
faster than we were flying."

Edgar shook his head in wonder at the memory.
"When we finally landed, all of us were all shaking
so badly we needed a good stiff drink just to settle
our nerves."

"So you abandoned your vow of abstinence?" Bram
asked with a smile.

"Damn right I did. First stop after landing and
using the men's room was the bar at the club. Two
shots of whiskey was my limit, but as I recall I never
stopped at one."

"How many trips did you make?" Bram asked.

"Thirty-two, if you count the last one."

He toyed with the handle of his mug, a faraway expression on his face, then continued. "In a strange way

I felt I was coming home when I reached Kunming. The truth is I'd spent far more time in China than I had in the United States, and more of it in South China than in San Angelo. I was on familiar turf, and I was now in uniform, an American officer, which gave me status and, by local standards, a fortune to spend.

"In basic training I'd been paid twenty-one dollars a month. Considering we were furnished bed, board and clothing, it was adequate to keep most guys on the edge of trouble. I received a small pay increase when I started pilot training, and since I didn't smoke or drink, I was able to save enough cash for the modest engagement ring I'd purchased for Evvie, but my pay was still far from enough to free her from Miss Hattie's.

"When I earned my wings and got my commission, my income skyrocketed to two hundred and fifty dollars a month. Just because I was angry at Evvie for what she was doing didn't change the fact that I loved her—passionately. I had one goal now, one obligation, one promise I had to keep—to rescue her from the bordello. Sir Galahad, remember?

"My plan was simple. I would send her two hundred dollars a month, every month. That would leave me fifty bucks or so for my own needs.

"There was no centralized pay system in those days, no direct deposit. We carried our pay records with us and got paid personally in cash. If we wanted to send money to someone other than immediate family, for which we could make out an allotment, we had to buy postal money orders and mail them.

"So when the paymaster showed up, I purchased a two-hundred-dollar money order and sent it to Evvie, with a solemn promise that I would be sending her the same every month. I also sent a twenty-dollar money order to Zeke as the first installment toward the two-hundred-buck debt I'd accumulated working for him.

"You can't imagine how proud of myself I felt. Evvie would be able to leave Miss Hattie's because of me. She wouldn't have to turn tricks anymore. She could stay home and help her mother, take care of the kids and wait for me. I had the ring I'd bought for her. Maybe I'd trade it in for a bigger one. Without question, the first thing I'd do when I got home would be to offer it to her and ask her to be my wife.

"In the meantime there was a war to fight.

"My days were busy. I spent most of my time flying the hump between India and China, delivering men and matériel to Kunming or distributing them to outlying locations.

"At the end of every mission I'd ask about the other crews and use that second drink to toast the ones who didn't make it. Every morning I'd wonder if this was the day I would become another statistic, another fatality without a tombstone."

"Yet you always got back into the cockpit," Bram observed.

"It was a matter of honor, son. When your country

is at war and your buddies are risking their lives, you can't do less. The only question in your mind is how well you'll acquit yourself when crunch time comes.

"I also had a more personal demon to contend with. I hadn't been with a woman since my last night with Evvie. There'd been opportunities, and God knows there'd been temptations, but whenever I got close to crossing the line with a willing babe, I'd look at the woman, picture Evvie and back away. Now I was in China, in completely different but familiar surroundings. I also realized Chinese women didn't remind me of Evvie, at least not as much as the girls back in the States did.

"So while other G.I.s were quibbling in pidgin English with bar girls and streetwalkers over prices for various personal services, I hightailed it to a palace of pleasure.

"The hazards of dallying with women of ill repute in Kunming were no different from what they were back home or anywhere else, the chief being venereal disease. China was in a terrible state, and prostitution, which was historically a legally recognized profession, was rampant because of all the military forces and displaced persons, both Chinese and foreign, wandering about the country. The number of transient partners a hooker might entertain had grown exponentially with the ravages of war and famine, so that engaging their services was even more of a danger. One way of limiting the risk of infection was to buy a girl's exclusivity.

"The House of the Eight Drunken Faeries—no, not

the kind you're thinking of…it's sometimes translated into English as the House of the Eight Immortals—had been a brothel long before my great-great-grandfather had been born. Chuang-Mu, the boss lady of the house, was impressed by my command of Chinese and was probably even more pleased with my status as an officer, albeit a mere second lieutenant. She offered me a special deal. For thirty dollars American a month, a girl would keep house for me, wash my clothes, cook my food and cater to my more personal requirements.

"Her name was Mei Lin. Chuang-Mu claimed she was fifteen, but a couple of remarks she let slip led me to suspect she was closer to my age, maybe even older. Men over there preferred their women young, so the girls lied about their age for as long as they could. Plus, the younger the girl, the less peril of infection.

"Beautiful Plum Jade—that's what her name meant—was, according to Chuang-Mu, the third daughter of a poor farmer in an outlying village who had been sold to the madam of the house only recently to pay family debts. She had a pretty, oval, porcelain face; long, shiny black hair; liquid dark brown eyes; and a long neck, much prized by Oriental men. She spoke with a soft, singsong voice that was pure seduction.

"She was terrified of me when we were introduced. Here she was, this petite thing under five feet, rail thin and probably not more than eighty pounds soaking wet, being paired up with this huge barbarian over six feet tall. I more than likely weighed twice as much as any of her Chinese or Japanese clients. Her hand, little more than the size of a child's, trembled when I held it in mine. I did my best to assure her I was a gentle giant. The fact that I spoke fluent Cantonese helped, but it was still a while before she was willing to trust me not to hurt her.

"Mei Lin was so sweet and delicate, and like all Oriental women in her circumstances, had been taught to be totally subservient to the man. She would do anything I asked of her and make me believe it was her greatest pleasure. It puffs a man up, let me tell you, being treated like a god. I never took advantage of it the way some men did, but I have to admit it was beguiling.

"I know what you're thinking, son. You're wondering if I felt guilty about cheating on Evvie."

Bram didn't say anything.

"Hell, yes, I felt guilty, but a man's libido has a habit of short-circuiting his conscience."

He lifted his coffee cup nervously, remembered it was empty and looked around. The waitress was busy at another table, her back to him.

"Let's walk around a bit," he said abruptly.

He rose stiffly from his wire-frame chair and set it under the edge of the table. They wandered to the back of the café and into what was actually the neighboring building. The exposed brick walls were covered with old oil-company signs—Esso, Sunoco, the Flying A— as well as car-license plates from a variety of states, several of them dating back to the 1920s.

Edgar scanned the assorted merchandise strewn

across hip-high counters and picked up a circular piece of perforated tin with folded-down wires on it.

"If I'd known people would someday want these things, I would have kept ours."

"What is it?" Bram asked.

"A toaster." He assembled the wires into a pyramid pattern. "You put bread on each side and set it on the gas burner. Just remember to turn the bread before it burns. Voilà! Toast."

"I think I'll stick with our pop-up."

The old man snickered. "Me, too."

They moved on.

"I'm sure Sarah will agree with me," Edgar commented quietly, though no one was nearby, "when I say people have a remarkable capacity for rationalizing their bad behavior. I imagine she mentally justified her actions as no more than giving satisfaction in exchange for remuneration her client was willing and able to pay, that she was merely fulfilling the terms of a personal-services contract, entered into freely by consenting adults. No one was hurt. A victimless crime."

Bram kept his head down, supposedly surveying the random collection of merchandise.

"Except now she's become the victim," the old man continued, "because what she did was not only against the law but frowned on by society. She'll carry that disgrace, if not the guilt, around with her for the rest of her life, son. Your job isn't so much to forgive her as it is to help her heal the scars.

"As for me," he added after a deep breath, "I used

all the classic excuses. I was a soldier at war. I might be killed at any time, therefore I deserved what pleasure I could find before my life ended. Was it true? Only that I might die. That didn't justify my violating a sacred trust, which is what love is. Did I comprehend that at the time? At my core I did. I loved Evvie. I owed her my fidelity. Then. Now. Always."

A minute went by. Bram moved around the end of the counter, picked up a metal frame about the size of a paperback and held it out to his grandfather. "Any idea what this is?"

His grandfather looked at it and chuckled. "That, my boy, is a razor-blade sharpener."

"A what?"

Edgar took the device and moved an inset carriage back and forth in its track. It clicked with precision. "You put the razor blade here, and run it across those leather surfaces to strop it. Razor blades were double edged back then, but they weren't stainless steel. The ones packaged in red were good for one shave. The blue blades lasted two, maybe three shaves, depending on how coarse a beard you had."

"Did this gadget work? Did it really sharpen them?"

"Never as good as new. Both kinds of blades were made of low-grade steel, so they didn't hold an edge for very long, and if you didn't dry them carefully after use, they'd be rusty the next time you picked them up." He put the relic back on the counter. "Great piece of nostalgia. Lousy way to shave."

They proceeded down the line. Edgar smiled at a

Howdy Doody lunch box beside a Hopalong Cassidy version.

"So did you take Mei Lin home with you?" Bram asked.

"I spent the night with her and was sorely tempted to, but in the light of morning I came to my senses. I loved Evvie. Getting laid was one thing. Setting up housekeeping was another. That didn't mean I didn't return to the House of the Eight Drunken Faeries on occasion to satisfy my carnal lusts."

"Did you ever tell Grandma about Mei Lin?" Bram asked.

Edgar shook his head. "Absolutely not."

He toyed with a few scattered objects. An old can opener, a potato peeler, a cheese slicer.

"I hope you're never unfaithful to your wife, son, but if you are, keep your damn mouth shut about it. Don't volunteer the information. If you get caught, well, that's a different matter. Lying then will only compound the problem. But for heaven's sake, don't think you can salve your conscience by hurting the person you love, which is exactly what confessing to infidelity does."

He lifted the lid of a gray cookie jar shaped like the head of an elephant and peeked inside. No cookies.

"You may think confession will make you feel better, but that's pure selfishness, the same vice that made you unfaithful in the first place. Confessing to your wife that you once robbed the corner grocery store is one thing. She'll no doubt be disappointed in you, but she's not the one you've injured, and there's a chance, if you make restitution, she might even respect you for your newfound honesty. But when you cheat on her, you can never make restitution, never. You're not just telling her you're weak—you're telling her she's inadequate and unworthy of your devotion. Maybe she'll forgive you for your weakness, but she won't ever feel the same about herself, and she'll never be able to completely trust you again. You both lose."

"But what about secrecy, Gramps?" Bram asked. "Doesn't that destroy marriages, too?"

"And that's the core of the problem with infidelity, son. You've put yourself in a no-win situation. You have to keep a secret from the very person who deserves your complete honesty unconditionally—for her peace of mind. You are free to confess every other deep dark secret you might have, but not that one, because no other offense will hurt her the way that one does."

They returned to the table in the coffee shop and the waitress reappeared and refilled their cups. After she left, Bram said, "Don't stop now, Gramps. I want to hear more about the war, about you and Gram."

Chapter 18

"It was a Monday afternoon in November," Evvie said, "two weeks from Thanksgiving... Let me begin again.

"Mom and I usually went food shopping together on my day off, but that Monday her rheumatism told her a storm was coming in, so she decided to stay home and finish the load of wash she'd started in the hope that there'd be enough time for it to dry before the rain hit. I returned and found my cousins playing in the neighbor's yard. Mom occasionally left them there if she had to go somewhere, but not generally when she was home. The neighbor lady wasn't in sight, probably attending to her own housework. Then I realized the wash Mom had been doing when I left was still soaking in the big galvanized tub outside, and the scrub board was right where it had been.

"I entered our back door into the kitchen, put my shopping bag on the table and called out, but got no answer. String beans sat in a colander in the sink, rinsed, waiting to be snapped. Potatoes were on the counter, a paring knife nearby. I called out again, but still received no response. Where could she have gone to? And why hadn't she left a note?

"Nervously I looked into the rooms downstairs and finally went up to my mother's bedroom. The door was closed. That was unusual. She rarely closed it, even at night, because she wanted to be able to hear the kids.

"I knocked. No answer.

"I turned the knob, inched the door open, whispered her name, but heard nothing.

"Sticking my head inside, I spied her curled up on her bed. Her eyes were half-open and watery, as though she was in a trance.

"I spoke to her, asked what was the matter. She didn't even acknowledge my presence. Now I was really scared. Had she had a heart attack, a stroke? Was she breathing?

"That was when I saw the yellow half sheet of paper clutched in her fist.

"My fingers shook as I pried it from hers. I moved over to the light of the window and stretched the paper out so I could read it. The words are burned into my memory.

The Secretary of War desires to express his deep regret that your son, Private Henry Douglas, was killed in action in defense of his country in North Africa November 10. Letter follows. The Adjutant General.

"I let out a shrill 'No' and collapsed onto the floor.

"It couldn't be. Not Henry. He couldn't be dead. It had to be a mistake.

"They'd gotten the name wrong.

"Not Henry. Not my big brother.

"As I lay on the bare wooden floor sobbing, my mind skipped about, playing tricks on me.

"I saw him as a confident seven-year-old, holding my hand as he escorted me to school for my first day in kindergarten, all the time assuring me I was going to have a swell time playing with the other children.

"I saw him as a young teenager, hoisting me on his shoulders at the swimming hole on our farm in Oklahoma when we played knights and castles with the neighbor's kids.

"I saw him a few years later, patiently explaining the mysteries of algebra to me, trying to put quadratic equations into terms my dull brain could comprehend. I eventually passed the test, even got a B in the course, but I never did understand what any of it was all about.

"I saw him in bib overalls on our tractor, plowing neat rows on Oklahoma fields that had become nothing but flyaway dust. Looking like a raccoon when he took off his goggles.

"I saw him in his uniform that last morning as we stood at the train station. So handsome, so proud, so confident. So alive. We'd laughed ourselves sick the night before, recounting how often we'd bugged each other, played practical jokes on people and giggled at their bewilderment.

"I recalled his arm around my shoulders—for the last time—telling me how glad he was that I was happy and how he hoped I would always be.

"Then I imagined him in a tuxedo, walking me down the aisle to Edgar. I visualized the proud, mischievous glint in his eyes and heard him say, 'Be happy.'

"I cried and cried, knowing I could never be completely happy again. I thought of all the conversations I still wanted to have with him. Would he have understood why I'd done what I had? I liked to think so. Now I would never be sure, and maybe that was the worst part of all. I'd never be able to ask him if I had done the right thing, or to ask his forgiveness if I hadn't.

"I'd loved my dad as only a young girl can love a father, but Henry had been my best friend. I'd always been able to depend on him. He couldn't be gone. He couldn't.

"Two days later we got a letter from Henry, and for a few minutes Mom and I succumbed to the illusion that the telegram had been in error. It wasn't. The letter was dated almost two weeks before he'd been killed.

"We read it and reread it. Did he know he was going to die? I didn't think so. He talked about all the things he wanted to do when he got home. Maybe we'd all go out to the golden land of California. With Dad gone there was nothing to keep us in Texas. He didn't want to return to Oklahoma. He remembered plenty of good times there, but not enough of them to call him back. California was the place. We'd all build a new life there."

"How old was your brother when he was killed?"

"Nineteen. Nowadays he wouldn't be old enough to drink."

Sarah bit her lip. "I'm so sorry."

"My brother's death brought more painful soul-searching and a stark question: How long could I play the role of a prostitute before I became one? Before it defined who I was?

"How long could I expect to escape getting the clap? I'd been very meticulous about my personal hygiene, but I also knew I'd been lucky. Future odds weren't in my favor.

"Since transferring overseas, Edgar had given up trying to persuade me in his letters to leave Miss Hattie's, but now, with Dad gone, I no longer had the recurring expense of having to send money to Carlsbad. The truth still remained, however, that we couldn't live exclusively on the money Mom earned washing and ironing. I'd also spent more money than was probably prudent giving my father a decent burial, but he and Uncle John still didn't have headstones.

"Nonetheless it was time for me to quit Miss Hattie's.

"The airfield the army had been building on the Metcalf place south of town was still under construction, but flight training had begun there even before the attack on Pearl Harbor, and now with the war fully under way, more and more troops were arriving. Administrative jobs previously performed by military personnel were being turned over to civilians. What's more, many of those jobs were going to women because there weren't enough men available to fill them.

"I decided to apply for whatever I could get.

"Miss Hattie hadn't been aggressive in recruiting me as a hooker, but she sure did try hard to talk me out of leaving. With so many doughboys—we hadn't started calling them G.I.s yet—and young officers assigned to the post, business had increased substantially. I was one of her best attractions, she acknowledged, and I could continue to be for several years, since I was only seventeen. She offered to increase my fee to three bucks. Again we would split it evenly. This represented a fifty percent pay raise for me.

"I'd turned to prostitution for the money, and only for the money, and here she was offering me more than I'd ever made. It tempted me, but not for long. No other jobs had been available when I started selling myself, and Edgar hadn't yet come into my life.

"I took the city bus out to Goodfellow Field and filled out a job application. I had to lie about my age, but no one questioned me when I said I was eighteen. Verifying that sort of thing wasn't as automatic or easy as it is today, and with mobilization in full swing, checking up on a girl wasn't a very high priority.

"I was hired as a file clerk in the supply room. The pay was twelve dollars a week, which represented more than a fifty percent pay cut even before Miss Hattie's promised pay raise, but the hours were regular, only forty versus the sixty to seventy I was routinely available at the bordello. Best of all I didn't have to worry anymore about VD or becoming pregnant, and I could hold my head up as a respectable defense worker.

"I talked it over with my mother, particularly the financial impact, but I had no doubt what she'd say. I'd gotten us past our biggest money crunch. We were eating better. There was extra food stored in the pantry. I'd bought new clothes for the kids and given Mom her first new dress in ten years. There was even a little cash put away in the Quaker oatmeal box in the back of a kitchen cabinet. We'd still have to be frugal, but we could live on my reduced income, plus Mom's washing.

"I retired from the trade."

"Mail delivery to and from India and China was, as you might imagine, less than punctual or reliable," Edgar continued. "A month had gone by since I'd dispatched my money orders to Evvie and Zeke, and I'd heard nothing back from either of them. Surely with the money I had sent, Evvie had left Miss Hattie's. Why hadn't she written to tell me the good news?

"Then I received a letter from Cousin Zeke—no word of that dough and the promise of more, which suggested he hadn't received it, because Zeke wasn't one to neglect the mention of money—informing me Evvie's brother had been killed in North Africa. The news stunned me. I'd never met Henry, but I knew Evvie was very close to him.

"I immediately sat down and wrote her a letter. Later that night, as I lay in bed and tried to go to sleep,

I was overwhelmed with guilt. I loved Evvie. I had no right to be having sex with other women. At least I hadn't brought Mei Lin home to live with me. But that didn't matter. I had criticized Evvie for letting other men use her, yet here I had hired—more than once— the services of a prostitute. I was disgusted with myself and ashamed. I vowed then I would never again be un- faithful to Evvie."

"Did you keep your pledge?" Bram asked.

"I never had sex with Mei Lin again," Edgar replied. "But I can't claim it was because I didn't want to."

"I arrived home on my first workday at the airfield feeling better about myself than I had in a long time to find a letter from Edgar waiting for me on the kitchen table. What could possibly make the day more perfect? I opened it and a money order tumbled to the floor. I picked it up. Two hundred dollars. I stared at it, my mouth hanging open, and sank onto a ladder-back chair, then started reading. Wait, let me get it."

Evvie disappeared inside the house and came back a few minutes later with a yellowed envelope. The thin paper inside it crinkled when she carefully unfolded it. She read:

I just heard from Cousin Zeke that your brother, Henry, was killed several weeks ago in North Africa. Dear God, Evvie, why didn't you tell me?

My first reaction was anger that you hadn't, but then I considered why you held back telling me this terrible news.

Sweetheart, you don't have to hide anything from me, and I hope you never will. I understand in this case you did it because you wanted to spare me this tragedy, and I love you for that. I know the pain you are suffering now is beyond anything you have ever felt before, and I would give my life to spare you that heartache, but please don't ever keep anything from me again. I want to share everything with you. Everything.

Right now you can't imagine ever feeling joy or pleasure again, but God willing, you will, and if it is in his plan, I will be part of that happiness. I love you, my sweetheart, beyond anything you can imagine, and it will be my life's work to make you happy.

I wish I had gotten to meet Henry and become his friend. It would have made the sadness and pain I feel right now even worse, but he was a part of you, and I would have liked for him to be a part of us, as well.

God bless you and your mother. May this miserable war be over soon, so I can come home and hold you in my arms and never let you go.

All my love always,

Edgar

P.S. I wish I could have started sending you these money orders sooner. Please write, sweetheart. I miss you so much and haven't heard from you in a long time. E.

Chapter 19

Evvie excused herself and went inside the house—Sarah assumed to put the letter away—but the old woman came back a minute later carrying a thick photograph album.

"I thought you might enjoy seeing some pictures," she said, setting the tapestry-covered volume on the glass-topped table.

"Oh, I'd love to." Sarah sat up.

Evvie pulled her chair closer to the young woman. "I guess these albums are going the way of the Model T now with computer imagery here, but I have to admit I prefer them to clicking a mouse."

She opened the heavily padded cover. The first few

pages were sepia tones, not dissimilar from the kinds Sarah had viewed in museum displays, brown prints mounted on thick cardboard. Evvie identified her grandparents and parents, then skipped forward to the late thirties and forties.

She turned the page and tapped a photo. "This is Henry."

Her brother was perhaps sixteen or seventeen. Clean-cut, boyish but with the man about to emerge. His smile had an impish quality, as if he'd just heard...or told a good joke. The small, white clapboard house in the background appeared in serious need of maintenance and paint.

"Nice-looking kid." Sarah pointed to the picture beside his. "Is that you?" A girl of maybe fifteen standing alone in a barren field.

"Right before we moved to Texas."

"No wonder your father wanted to load his shotgun. You were gorgeous." In spite of the ill-fitting dress and windblown hair. "Wow." Sarah surveyed the old woman's aged face. Lips thinner of course. Bone structure more pronounced. But the essential beauty undiminished. "You really haven't changed."

Evvie laughed and practically blushed. "Why, thank you, my dear. Just six or seven decades older."

Sarah paged farther in the album. "Do you have any pictures of..."

"Miss Hattie?" Evvie shook her head. "She never allowed herself to be photographed."

Sarah found a picture of an unsmiling woman in a

suit she figured was probably taken in the late forties or early fifties.

"Is this your mother?"

Evvie nodded.

"You look like her. She was a very pretty woman."

"She wouldn't have agreed," Evvie said, "but my dad always thought she was. He said I took after her. I could never see the resemblance myself until I turned forty, then I stared into the mirror one morning and found my mother staring back at me. It was a bit disconcerting."

"How did she cope with your brother's death once the shock of it wore off?"

"The way she dealt with most things—silently. My mother wasn't a cold woman," Evvie added, "but she was a very private person, rarely exchanged intimacies or showed her feelings. Within a year she'd lost her home, her husband and her son, and her daughter had become a prostitute.

"She grieved, dried her tears, became more set in her ways and focused on Uncle John's kids, who weren't even related to her by blood. Did a good job of raising them, too, but something died inside her that November day in '42. Over her remaining years she laughed and sang and did all the things people are expected to do, but she was never quite the same. The smiles and cheerfulness after that couldn't disguise the deeper sadness in her eyes."

"She didn't remarry?"

Evvie shook her head. "I doubt she even gave it a

thought, and to be honest I can't remember a single man ever showing the least interest in her. She was liked and respected, she had a small circle of friends, but none I would ever have called close. Even when, later in life, she got involved in church and charity work, she projected a reserve that didn't invite intimacy."

Sarah was disappointed. "Your getting out of the business must have been a relief for both of you."

"You can't imagine how good it felt to leave there. No one had been mean to me. I can't claim to have been abused—with that one exception—or ever taken advantage of. I'd been fortunate, really. I hadn't contracted any diseases or gotten pregnant. I'd even made some good friends among the girls. I had done what I did willingly enough, but I truly hated it, hated the feeling of being dirty and afraid. Most of all I hated what it was doing to Edgar and me. I understood his outrage, his shame. I accepted that as my fault, not his."

Evvie smiled. "My pulse beat faster when I sat down to write my letter to him, announcing I'd finally left Miss Hattie's. I felt as if a great weight had been lifted from my heart, that I could breathe again. I renewed my love, promised to be waiting for him when he came home, and said that I hoped it would be soon."

"You were lucky you could just walk away," Sarah commented. "My name was published in the paper, and I caught holy hell from people about it."

"Oh, there were a couple of momentary setbacks," Evvie noted. "Two men at the airfield recognized me. One asked if I was freelancing. I said no. He nodded, walked away and never brought up the subject again. The other got nasty and threatened to have me fired if I didn't put out for him. I reminded him about the scar on his left buttock and asked what his wife would say when she found out I was familiar with certain intimate details of his anatomy. He backed off fast."

Sarah laughed. "I bet he did."

"I kept a sharp eye on him for a long time, though. I'd threatened him, made him feel vulnerable, which in turn made him dangerous. I reckoned he'd cause trouble for me if he got a chance, but I must have scared him enough, because he kept his distance from me after that and never bothered me again."

Sarah saw a picture in the album of a heavyset man with a cigar in his mouth, wearing a bold plaid sport jacket. "That has got to be Cousin Zeke."

Evvie chuckled. "He was a character. A used-car salesman with a heart of gold. Well, polished brass, anyway. He liked to play the tough guy, and I suppose under the right circumstances he could be, but I never felt threatened by him. On the contrary, I always felt safe with him."

Sarah casually paged through the album.

"After the scandal broke about our sorority," she said, "I had to hang around for a couple of months until graduation. It was the pits. Between propositions and foul-mouthed insults I was miserable and got out of there as soon as I could, but you stayed here. Wasn't it tough always wondering when someone was going to bring up your past?"

"I didn't have much choice, my dear. Fortunately people had plenty of other things to talk about. The war dominated most people's interests. Newspapers were full of stories about the battles being fought in Europe and the Pacific. There were reports of German subs spotted off the east coast, of Japanese subs off the west. Spies were picked up on beaches. Japanese Americans were being forced into detention camps in California, and of course there were the casualty reports. Telegrams announcing the death or wounding of servicemen from San Angelo were starting to arrive. The Western Union delivery boy was the most dreaded person in town."

Sarah gazed at a picture of a family picnic in a field, a woody station wagon sitting off to the side, tall mountains in the background. Evvie, Edgar and three young children on a blanket. "Did you ever get out to California?"

"Years later, to visit an old army buddy of Edgar's, his radio man. I could certainly understand why my brother had taken to the place, but the Golden State held no attraction by then. For me it represented a land of shattered dreams."

Evvie sipped her cordial. "The war brought prosperity of a kind," she said to change the subject. "Defense jobs were available at decent pay. National unemployment dropped to zero. Still, having a steady income didn't mean people were living well. Lack of cash now gave way to lack of goods. The list of items that required ration stamps kept growing. Sugar. Coffee. Gasoline. Rubber products, especially automobile tires. Meat. Cheese. Even fat. Canned goods were eventually put on the list, as well.

"Having the coupons and money to buy rationed or even nonrationed items didn't mean they were available, either. Grocery stores simply ran out. Meat, especially. This is cattle country, but there were times when finding a piece of beef was next to impossible at any price. In other cases, barter replaced cash, and a thriving black market of scarce commodities at exorbitant rates grew up quickly.

"Mom continued to take in laundry, mostly for military officers. I went back to sewing at night and on weekends, this time altering uniforms, sewing on insignia and patches. I didn't miss the irony that if the war had come a little earlier I would still be a virgin."

"The morning after I decided to cease calling on Mei Lin," Edgar went on, "I was given a mission to deliver aircraft parts to Kunming and pick up six G.I.s who were being transferred to another outfit. We were flying over eastern Burma, when a couple of Zeros came at us from out of nowhere.

"I heard a muffled pop, and before I could figure out what was happening, I'd lost power in number-two engine, and it started spewing black smoke. I gave the order to bail out, but it was already too late for that. We were losing speed and altitude fast. The only thing left was to ride it in.

"Thank God we hadn't reached the high mountains yet. The landscape below us was green jungle interspersed with patches of cultivation. I headed for the nearest open field. Stan, my copilot, and I managed to belly-land the crippled plane in the middle of a paddy.

"I checked myself over and decided I was uninjured, but we had casualties.

"Smoke was filling the fuselage. We had to get the hell out of there fast. The able-bodied struggled to help the injured. It was an excruciating process, but within a few minutes we were all moving toward a line of trees on top of an embankment. Then the Gooney Bird exploded, knocking us all down, sending an orange-and-black plume high into the sky, and of course marking our location.

"Soaking wet, we moved away from the blazing wreck toward what appeared to be a windbreak between flooded paddies.

"I tried to figure out where the devil we were, and what we were going to do next, but I didn't get time to speculate, much less devise a plan. A truckload of Japanese soldiers showed up on the road at the top of the levee. Except for the .45-caliber handguns Stan and I carried, we had no weapons to defend ourselves. Resistance would have been foolhardy and suicidal.

"They loaded us onto the truck none too gently, seeming to take glee at the injured screaming in pain.

"My Japanese wasn't as fluent as my Chinese, but I was easily able to follow what they were jabbering about. I was tempted to talk to them but then realized I could probably learn more from them if they didn't know I understood what they were saying, so I kept my mouth shut.

"They drove us to a small military compound and herded us into a bamboo hut. At that point I wasn't confident of anything, except that we were in deep trouble. I was twenty-one years old, a second lieutenant and the officer in charge. Crunch time had arrived.

"Would I live to see Evvie again?

"We received a wooden bucket of not very clean water that night, but no food. No interrogation, either, which convinced me none of them spoke English, especially after I'd heard the sergeant say he had radioed regional headquarters and they were sending an English-speaking officer.

"When morning arrived, I was concerned about Albert, one of the mechanics. He'd been ambulatory the afternoon before, but I'd heard him moan during the night. When I went over to him, he told me he'd gotten bruised in the crash, but that he would be fine. Not long after that his moaning stopped, and I figured he'd fallen asleep.

"A Japanese captain appeared on the scene.

"'What's wrong with him?' he asked me in English.

"'He's dead.' Albert must have ruptured his kidneys, maybe other organs, as well, and had bled out internally. The pain had to have been excruciating, but the nineteen-year-old bore it in silence.

"The captain ordered two of his men to remove the body, which they did unceremoniously.

"Then the captain ordered me to follow him."

Chapter 20

"On December 28,1942, three days after Christmas, Zeke received a copy of the letter that had been sent to Edgar's parents by the War Department informing them their son was officially missing in action. Zeke brought it to the house.

"I read it several times. He and his crew had gone down over rugged enemy territory. The letter implied, though it didn't explicitly state, that they had probably all perished.

"That was what my mother believed, and it sent her deeper into the depression created by Dad's and Henry's deaths. That was what Zeke thought, too, and it brought tears to his eyes.

"I refused to accept it. Edgar had to be alive. He

had to. Surely the Lord hadn't sent me to Miss Hattie's so I could meet him, only to take him away from me.

"Since I didn't want to be seen anywhere near Miss Hattie's, I called my friend Rosie from work the next day and arranged to meet her that evening over by old Fort Concho. We could stroll the quiet streets there and talk.

"'He's probably dead,' she said after I told her about the letter.

"'I don't believe it.' I was certain my next statement would draw scorn, but I felt compelled to say it anyway. 'I would know.'

"Rosie didn't laugh but she did stop and look at me with pity on her face. 'That's a very romantic notion, Evvie, that there's some sort of spiritual bond between the two of you. It might work in books and movies, but it doesn't in real life.'

"'I would know,' I repeated, fighting off tears of frustration.

"'Honey,' Rosie said, taking my hand, 'you have to be realistic. If you aren't, it'll only make matters worse and you'll drive yourself mad. What will your mother and the children do then?'

"'He's not dead.' I was adamant. 'He's not. Just because his plane crashed doesn't mean he was killed. He and his men could have survived.'

"'That isn't likely.'

"'I don't care. He isn't dead. He isn't.'

"He might be injured, though. Suppose he'd been wounded. Suppose he was maimed or blind. Still, if he was alive, that was all that mattered. If he came back crippled, I'd help him and care for him.

"'Maybe he was taken prisoner by the Japanese,' I suggested.

"'Then he's as good as dead,' Rosie declared. 'You've read the stories about Corregidor and Bataan. That was before we started bombing the hell out of Tokyo. After all the losses they've suffered, I doubt the Japanese are inclined to treat American POWs very nicely.'

"'Why are you doing this?' I shouted, backing away. 'I thought you were my friend. I thought you'd understand.'

"She came forward, compassion in her eyes, and put her arm across my shoulders. 'I am your friend, honey, and I do understand—really, I do—but things don't always work out the way we want them to.'

"As if I wasn't already aware of that.

"After a minute she linked her arm with mine and we continued our walk past the big stone building that had once been the fort's commissary into the quiet residential area behind it.

"'I know you love him, Evvie,' she said, 'and he loved you when he left, but you have to face the fact that he'll be a different person when he comes back— if he comes back. A man can't go through what he has and not be changed.'

"'What do you mean?' I asked, not at all happy with this new tack. I was sorry now I'd called her. Rosie wasn't helping one bit. I'd wanted sympathy and support. Instead I felt more alone than ever.

"'If he comes back, he'll be a war hero, and you'll still be a whore.'

"I pulled away from her and yelled at her. 'Don't say that. I'm not. Not anymore.'

"'Nothing you ever do will change what you were, Evvie,' she said quietly. I could hear empathy and sadness in her voice. 'You saw what happened to me.' She linked her arm with mine again, and we resumed our walk. 'I thought I'd found my Prince Charming, too, the hero who was going to rescue me from my life of shame and make me a respectable woman, but it didn't work out that way. I think George genuinely cared for me. He doesn't stop by anymore for a piece of the action, but we're still friends. The problem was that even when it was just the two of us he couldn't forget he'd been one of many, and his family sure didn't welcome me as a sinner who'd been saved.'

"'Didn't he trust you?'

"'It wasn't a matter of trust. It was more like…he wasn't sure if I was making love to him or just letting him screw me. You know what? He was right. Sometimes I wasn't sure, either.'

"'Didn't he—'

"'Shiver my quiver?' She laughed. 'Sure he did, and when he didn't, I faked it. Maybe that was the problem and my big mistake. Maybe he figured out I was only pretending. Doesn't do much for a man's ego when he can't satisfy his woman. A man likes to think she needs him, can't get along without him, can't be satisfied by anyone but him.'

"I need Edgar, I thought. I can't get along without him. Nobody will ever satisfy me the way he does.

"I had faked it all the time with other guys but never with Edgar. I loved him too much to deceive him. Besides, the way he made love to me, the way he aroused me… There was no necessity to fake anything with him.

"'Did you love George?' I asked Rosie.

"She shrugged noncommittally. 'In my own way. I certainly cared for him. Still do, I guess. I tried to make him happy. I was grateful to him for wanting me, and I would never have messed around on him. Perhaps if we'd moved away, started over where no one knew us, he could have let go of my past, but San Angelo is his home. He wouldn't leave the ranch he'd grown up on, that his daddy had grown up on, and I wasn't about to ask him to. I doubt that was the real issue, anyway.'

"The problem was Rosie, I concluded, and took as much consolation from that as I could. She thought of herself as a prostitute. But I didn't think of myself that way. In spite of what I'd done, I didn't associate the real me with the person who had sold herself to be used as a sex object by men. That woman had been someone else, an alter ego. Maybe I was being unkind, presuming Rosie liked being a prostitute. She and most of the other girls hadn't entered the profession because they wanted to, and if they could go back and make a different choice they would, but I suspected Rosie got off having sex with different men now. A lot of girls learned to, and it would be unfair to condemn them for it. Why shouldn't they take pleasure in what they did? I just wasn't one of them, and I had no desire to be.

"'If Edgar ever does come back,' Rosie said, 'he's going to want a new life, a life that may not include you.'

"I hated her at that moment. Hated her because she was putting into words the very doubts that had been eating away at me for months.

"Once a whore, always a whore, whether you were still turning tricks or not.

"'He's not like that,' I argued, but even I could hear the lack of conviction in my voice. 'He loves me.'

"'I hope you're right, honey, but you better prepare yourself. If he's still alive, if he comes back physically sound, he'll be a changed man. The girl he wanted when he left here may not be the woman he wants when he returns.'

"Suppose Rosie was right. Suppose Edgar decided he didn't want a former prostitute for a wife. What would I do then? How would I ever live without him?"

Bram shook his head. "I had no idea you'd been a POW, Gramps. You never talk about your war experiences."

"Most of them I'd just as soon forget, son, and you had to be there to understand what it was like. I'm not even sure why I'm telling you about them now."

"I hope you don't stop." On a lighter note, he added, "Maybe we ought to call you the modest generation, as well as the greatest generation."

"It's not modesty," the old man said without humor.

"In war men do things they would never even consider doing in peacetime, things that on reflection scare the hell out of them. It's not like in the movies. Firing a rifle blindly into a stand of trees and seeing a target three hundred yards away tumble to the ground is one thing. Being close enough to hear the scream of pain you've inflicted is another, and looking into the eyes of that other human being as he dies… Those images can haunt a man for the rest of his life.

"You ask yourself questions for which there are no adequate answers. Did you do the right thing? Even if you conclude that militarily and even morally you did—it doesn't stop you from wondering about the other poor sap. Did he have a family? Parents, siblings, a wife, kids? What were his ambitions in life? Why did he die and you live?

"So you come home and try to put it all behind you. Compartmentalization, the shrinks call it, but those experiences never completely go away. They pop up and say boo when you least expect it, and the circle of demons surrounds you all over again."

Edgar clamped his jaw, sorry he'd brought up the subject.

"Do you ever have nightmares about what happened?"

The old man bent his head slightly to the side and lifted one shoulder in a vague shrug. "Not as often as I used to. I had a lot of them right after the war. Waking up to find Evvie beside me made all the difference in the world."

After a brief, silent pause, Bram asked, "Will you go on with your story, Gramps?"

Chapter 21

"Exhausted, weak from hunger," Edgar continued, "the seven of us who were still alive were loaded three days later onto a canvas-topped truck and roughly transported about fifteen miles to a camp that held maybe a hundred other prisoners, mostly Brits and a few Aussies. After six months there they were in sorry shape. All of them were scrawny. Some had running sores. A few were using improvised splints, canes and crutches. Several had limbs missing or rendered useless.

"Food was scarce. A single bowl of boiled rice twice a day. If we found weevils in it, we welcomed them as protein. A few vegetables, mostly pieces of fibrous yam, occasionally small portions of pork or water buffalo. If we caught a rat or other varmint, we threw it into the stew pot, as well.

"Our compound was one of a dozen labor camps strung out through the mountains. The Japanese were struggling to build and maintain roads to get their supplies through, just as we were.

"The movie about the bridge over the River Kwai is a fantasy. I assure you, we didn't whistle while we worked. We felled trees with hand axes and saws. We dug trenches with spades and as often with our bare hands. If you didn't get out of the way of a falling tree fast enough, too bad. The coup de grâce in the back of the head was the best you could hope for. If you collapsed from exhaustion into a trench or tried to catch a moment's rest in one, it was likely to become your grave.

"My crew and I had crash landed in the fall of '42. By that same time in '43 only half of our original labor-camp contingent was left. Of us seven Americans, only five were still alive. The sadism of our guards was unrelenting and insanely gratuitous. Men were punched, pistol whipped, stabbed, kicked, garroted and shot for no apparent reason. We despised them, not as enemies, but as cowards. Physically we weren't worthy opponents, but I guess it was the image of the big, strong Westerner that they were taking their frustrations out on.

"My copilot, Stan, was killed in an allied air raid. We were now down to four.

"One of them was Sparky, our radio operator. In quiet moments of exhaustion we talked about home and of course the girls we left behind. I told him all about Evvie, about her soft chestnut hair, her green eyes, the tantalizing shape of her mouth, the mellow sound of her voice, especially when she laughed. I didn't tell him what it felt like to make love to her, but I thought about it, and of course I left out the part about Miss Hattie's.

"I rarely thought of Mei Lin, and never in a sexual way, only to wonder what had happened to her after I left. She would undoubtedly remain in her war-torn land with little hope of her life ever significantly improving.

"As time went on and each day became a new struggle for survival, things that had once seemed so important gradually lost their significance. I sought consolation in the fact that Evvie was home safe. Don't get me wrong, son, I still wanted her out of that damn brothel, but I ceased to think of her in terms of Miss Hattie's, and my anger, my wounded pride, slowly dissipated. When I returned to San Angelo, I'd change things, I resolved, because there I'd be a man in charge of my own fate.

"While I dreamed on about my life with Evvie, Sparky rhapsodized about his fiancée, Patsy, back in San Jose, California. In fact, he had a picture of her. Carrying personal items like photos and letters on combat missions was strictly forbidden, but Sparky had received this snapshot just before we'd taken off and had stuck it in his pocket. He'd managed somehow to hide it from our captors, and he showed it to me. A little tattered, but I could make out a pretty girl with long black hair and dark eyes. She was holding a puppy and smiling happily into the camera.

"I envied him having that picture, but I also warned him to be very careful. It wasn't worth getting shot over.

"Nineteen-forty-three slipped into 1944. From eavesdropping on conversations between guards and officers I knew the war wasn't going well for them, but our little contingent wasn't doing all that great, either. Each day now started with a burial detail.

"In January of '45, they marched us for days to a seaport where we were loaded onto a cargo ship. One hundred and fifty-seven of us were crowded into the dank bowels of a rusty old tub, given a few buckets of water, no food and a single bucket for our waste. Conditions were so crowded we had to take turns lying down to sleep.

"Five days later we were offloaded at the Japanese harbor of Fukuoka on the north coast of the southern island of Kyushu. Twenty-six men had died, their bodies tossed overboard. We were marched to an internment camp beyond a military airstrip at the end of the peninsula that guarded Hakata Bay. They had a low-grade, brown-coal mine there and that was where we were going to spend our last days—as slave labor."

"So you worked in the coal mine?" Bram asked.

"They wanted me to. The problem was my size. Most Japanese men in those days weren't more than five-four. I was six-two, a giant by their standards and too big to fit into the low, narrow mine tunnels they'd dug to extract coal by hand.

"The part of Japan we were in was rural and agricultural. On our march from the port to the camp we'd passed flooded rice paddies, ready for planting. They reeked of the night soil used for fertilizer. All the houses were small and thatched. This was the boondocks by Japanese standards. I doubt much had changed in five hundred years.

"The camp commandant, an army major, decided to dole out me and a few of the other bigger fellows as free labor to the farmers and fishermen in the little village of Saitosaki. Sure, we could have overpowered our peasant hosts, but what would that have accomplished? They weren't the enemy, and where could we have escaped to? We were on a narrow peninsula, which limited our flight options, and Westerners our size could hardly hide among the teeming population of Fukuoka. Technically, I suppose, we were helping the enemy, but these weren't armament factories. We weren't directly contributing to the war effort, and we could always destroy the harvest later, if it became necessary. In the short term, we had to eat, too."

"How were you treated?"

Edgar let out a quiet snort. "Actually, Seki and his wife, Kuniko, were terrified of me. At first, at least. Understandable. He was about fifty, too old for army service. Plus he had a bum leg. Limped badly. He didn't stand more than five-one or -two. His wife, who was probably ten years younger, was even smaller. Over time I learned they had two sons. One had been killed while serving aboard a ship. The other was in the army somewhere. They hadn't heard from him in a long time and were afraid he was dead, too. Seki's mother lived with them, as well. She was over seventy.

"God, they were a pitiful lot. Emaciated elves rather than full-size adults. We all worked and ate together, slept in the same room. Even bathed together. After they realized I meant them no harm, they were models of politeness and decorum."

"So did you speak to them in Japanese?"

"I didn't want to take a chance on word getting back to camp officials, so I continued to play dumb, occasionally mispronouncing words I pretended to have picked up along the way."

Bram glanced over at this grandfather. "It sounds like you grew fond of them."

Edgar smiled. "I did. They were simple, hardworking people, uneducated and unpolitical. Then one night everything changed."

"I guess that broke up your friendship with Rosie," Sarah observed. She and Evvie were strolling toward the barn and corral area to check on Daedulus, the young colt Bram had earlier remarked on.

The old woman smiled as she walked along the white rail fence separating them from the broad pasture. "I stayed angry with her for a long time. Her blunt assessment of the situation had undermined what little confidence I had in myself. Worse still, she'd made me begin to doubt Edgar. He was too good for me. I'd known that from the start, yet he'd never made me feel like a soiled dove when I was with him. Only loved, cherished. I ached to feel that way again."

The not-unpleasant smell of horses greeted them as they drew closer to the steel barn that was in the process of being faced on the outside with creamy-white Austin stone. Sarah was a city girl and always found the ranch fascinating.

They stepped into the dim building. Horse stalls lined both sides of a wide concrete aisle. Each of the sliding doors had wooden placards with names deeply etched into them: Birdsong, Lottie, Rêve de Coeur, Fyffe, Annie, on one side. Cinco de Mayo, Mack, Odin, Conrad, on the other. At the end, in the oversize last stall usually reserved for stallions, stood Isabel and her colt, Daedulus. The mare came up to the gate, her curious offspring following. Evvie made soothing sounds as she reached in and tickled the mother's nose.

"Life ground on," Evvie told Sarah. "The economic depression was over, but the hardships weren't, except now we felt they had a purpose." From the back pocket of her baggy jeans, she extracted one of the carrots she'd brought from the kitchen and offered it to the mare. The colt was still nursing.

"We had scrap-metal drives. Kids collected tin cans—they were all made of steel back then—even the foil wrappers from chewing gum and cigarette packs. We collected old rags and paper to be made into more paper, gathered wooden coat hangers to deliver to the soldiers in the barracks at the airfield, because all the metal ones had to go for scrap. We baked cookies, packed them in unsalted popcorn to send to the boys overseas. We supported one another, cried together when anyone received word that a son or brother or father had been killed, wounded or had gone missing, and we had letter-writing campaigns to let the troops know they were always in our minds."

Daedulus stood now beside his dam within reach of the people on the other side of the barrier. Slowly the old woman introduced her hand, let the colt sniff it, even more slowly and lovingly tickled the young animal's nose, then moved her fingers up and rubbed his ears.

"Want to pet him?" she asked Sarah.

Sarah nodded. "Can I?"

Evvie talked her through the process, emphasizing not to make any sudden moves. The young woman's face glowed when she felt the velvety softness between the colt's nostrils. Again following directions, she stroked the horse's jaw.

A few minutes later they moved away, and Evvie went down the line, giving each of the horses a piece of carrot and a fond touch.

"They were terrible times," she said as they exited the building. "Filled with so much uncertainty. But the worst of times bring out the best in people, too, like the days immediately following 9/11. We banded together. We weren't just a community united. We were all part of one big family."

Outside, they circled the barn. Evvie nodded with approval at the progress being made on siding the metal building.

"I continued to work at the airfield," she said. "I was happy there. I felt I was really contributing to the war effort."

They began their journey back to the house on the hill.

"The supply room was across the street from the hospital and I got into the habit of walking over every day at lunchtime to visit with the troops. Many of them were from West Texas. This was their last stop before being discharged. I wrote letters and penny postcards for the out-of-towners who weren't able to do it for themselves, read them the correspondence they received from home and occasionally made collect telephone calls to families and girlfriends for guys who weren't yet ambulatory."

"I'm sure they appreciated it," Sarah said, "but it must have been hard, encountering all those wounded men."

"It was. They were so young, the majority of them in their early twenties. The good part was most would fully recover and get on with the rest of their lives, but there were heartbreaking cases, too, young men—some still teenagers—with permanent disabilities. Missing limbs. Blind. Paraplegic. Badly burned and scarred. Some would have to go through weeks and months of painful rehabilitation and multiple surgeries before they could be released, and still their lives would never be the same."

"And all the time I bet you kept thinking about Edgar," Sarah said quietly, "picturing him in one of those beds."

Evvie moved more slowly uphill, but she didn't stop.

"How could I not, my dear? I looked at these fellas, young men around his age, and worried if Edgar had lost an arm or leg, if he was blind, if he was going to be confined to a wheelchair or even a bed for the rest of his life."

She turned to Sarah. "I would have attended to his needs regardless of his condition, but I had to wonder how he would cope. Would he grow bitter if he couldn't walk, if he couldn't see? Would he eventually just give up and die?"

They arrived at the house. It was cooler in the shade of the porch now.

"We have time," Evvie said, "for another pot of tea before the men get back."

Sarah gathered up the liqueur bottle and glasses and carried them to the kitchen, where Evvie filled the kettle and put it on the stove.

"You said they were from West Texas," Sarah noted. "So did any of them recognize you from before, and did any of them proposition you?"

Evvie laughed. "They were men, my dear. Of course they flirted with me, but not because of Miss Hattie's. Hormones. The guys who made passes were the ones on the road to recovery. It was definitely a positive sign."

The kettle whistled. Evvie prepared the tea. Sarah carried the tray, and they retraced their steps to the patio.

"But I was telling you about Rosie," Evvie said as she poured the hot tea.

Chapter 22

Evvie squeezed a wedge of lemon into her tea, added a scant teaspoon of sugar and stirred it.

"A few months after my disastrous meeting with Rosie," she continued, "I was over at the hospital during my lunch hour when one of the new patients recognized me. He didn't say from where, but we both knew. He was older than the others, in his mid-thirties. He'd been shot in the gut. The bullet had passed through his abdomen and severed his spinal cord, leaving him paraplegic. We talked for a while, and he asked about Rosie. Turned out he'd been one of her regulars.

"That afternoon I called her from the office and told her about Otis and that he'd inquired after her. She remembered him and said she'd try to stop by to say hello to him later that day."

Evvie smiled. "And she did. That afternoon, and the next afternoon, and the afternoon after that. Six months later they were married."

"I hope you're going to tell me this marriage lasted, that they lived happily ever after," Sarah said.

"Very happy. She was absolutely devoted to him. Unfortunately, ever after didn't last very long. He died suddenly one night about three years later of a cerebral hemorrhage."

"That's so sad. Surely she didn't go back to Miss Hattie's."

Evvie shook her head. "It was closed by then, shut down by the Texas Rangers. She told me she wouldn't have gone back anyway. It would have been an insult to Otis's memory."

"So how did she make a living?"

"She inherited a share of his family's ranch."

"Oh. Well, that was nice. At least she didn't have to work anymore."

"But she did. Otis's mother had never approved of her—for obvious reasons—and made it clear she thought her devotion to Otis had been nothing more than an act, that she was just waiting for him to die so she could get his money. Well, Rosie proved her wrong. She waived her portion of the family ranch and walked away, got a job in a local restaurant and waited on tables for the next thirty years."

Sarah was astounded. "Wow, to walk way from a fortune like that…"

"She told me those three years were the happiest she'd ever experienced, and that the memory of them would be enough to sustain her for the rest of her life."

The two women sat in silence for several minutes, each in her own thoughts.

"You said the Texas Rangers closed Miss Hattie's," Sarah finally said. "When was that?"

"Twice, actually. The first time was in 1947. By the last year of the war, the post commander at Goodfellow Field had put the place off-limits to all military personnel. A few violated the ban, of course, but business still took a nosedive, and after the war there'd been a culture shift. Returning G.I.s weren't interested in just getting laid." Evvie chuckled. "I'm not saying they would turn down a good piece of ass, mind you, but most of them were seeking more than a one-night— or one-hour—stand. With the economy booming, they wanted to settle down, marry, raise families and move on with their lives, and the women they came back to weren't nearly as passive as the girls they'd left behind.

"Women had found the kind of independence and self-assurance during the war they hadn't had before. They were beginning to regard themselves as men's equals rather than their subordinates, and definitely not their inferiors. After all, women hadn't just held jobs previously performed by men. They'd helped win the war by doing them well, and with this proof that they could compete in the workplace arose the realization they were also entitled to the same benefits men got. Equal wages. Respect. The right to handle their own affairs."

She laughed and raised her cup to her lips. "My, my, I didn't mean to get so philosophical." She took a sip of her tea and returned the cup to the saucer.

"I've gotten off track. There was really a much simpler explanation for why Miss Hattie's business fell off. Elmo, the old black man who had done all the common-area cleaning, as well as a variety of minor maintenance chores, had died a few years earlier. Finding a replacement with the same level of skill and dedication had proved impossible, and hiring individual jobbers to do all those different tasks was both expensive and haphazard. By the time the Rangers barged into the place in '47 it was beginning to look pretty seedy. Shutting it down was as much for health-and-safety reasons as moral."

"So what happened to the girls?" Sarah asked.

"Some of them went on the circuit to ply their trade. Mable, the gal with the baby, was rejoined by her husband after he was released from the TB sanitarium. They moved to New Mexico, settled down, had a couple more kids and led a very ordinary, upright life.

"Eula Mae Fargus, Miss Kitty, married a local rancher, became a homemaker and raised seven children. She died about ten years ago, the revered matriarch of a large and prominent family."

"Sounds like a happy ending to me," Sarah commented.

Evvie's smile turned into a grin. "Dorothea Kraus, the one we called Miss Blue, went back to school, got her teaching certificate and taught elementary school in San Antonio. Retired as principal twenty-five years later."

Sarah grinned. "Good for her. And Goldie. What about Goldie?"

Evvie chuckled. "Another rancher, an older married man, developed an attachment for her and asked her to become his exclusive mistress in exchange for his promise to remember her in his will. She did. He didn't. When he died a few years later, she found herself bereft. By then the brothel had been closed several years. She approached Miss Hattie, who still owned the property, bought it from her and reopened it as the new madam. Still called it Miss Hattie's, though. That was in late '49 or early '50. But, as I said, times had changed. Bawdy houses were no longer in vogue. In June of '52 the Rangers shut it down for the second time, this time for good.

"Goldie was arrested, spent thirty days in the local jail and left town. Heard she went to Las Vegas, but I lost track of her after that."

"And Miss Hattie herself? What became of her?"

"Miss Hattie was a crafty businesswoman. Over the years she'd acquired quite a few pieces of property around town. When the Rangers padlocked her door, she set up a real-estate agency and continued to rake in money for the next twenty years. Died at the age of ninety-two, leaving behind an estate estimated to be worth over ten million dollars. She had no family. It all went to a national foundation for abused and battered children."

"The madam with the heart of gold," Sarah noted a little cynically.

Evvie smiled. "Something like that. She never talked about herself, and I often wondered what her background was."

"Okay," Sarah said, straightening up in her chair. "Enough about them. What I'm really dying to find out is what happened between you and Edgar. Obviously he didn't die in the war, and he wasn't maimed. So tell me about your reunion."

"After three months of living with my Japanese family," Edgar said, "I had come to respect and admire them. They worked hard, from sunup to after sundown and received few rewards for their labors, except for one thing. They had each other.

"They didn't use terms of endearment. It wasn't part of their culture. Physical contact was likewise limited. But it didn't matter. They shared a communion of spirit that made me envious.

"I kept picturing Evvie and imagining what it would be like to share a lifetime with her, to raise a family. I was starved for what these two people had, a bond that lifted them above their hardships, that gave them the strength and perseverance to keep going even in the face of unbearable hardships, losses and sorrows.

"I pictured Evvie in the plain cotton dresses she wore to and from her mother's house, her chestnut hair bouncing off her shoulders, her green eyes warm, inquisitive. This was the real Evvie, not the one in Miss Hattie's parlor, wearing provocative outfits and cosmetics.

"I dreamed of her at night and woke up in the morning still exhausted from the previous day's work but smiling nevertheless at the sweet memory or Evvie's kisses. The way she touched me. The wonder I felt when I ran the tip of my finger along the warm, smooth curve of her skin.

"The war would end, I kept telling myself. I would go home and be with her again.

"Then something happened that changed my life.

"We'd put in another fourteen-hour day, eaten a meal that didn't come close to approximating the calories we'd expended, drunk our last cup of weak green tea in the fading light and settled down for the night. Sometime later, as I was drifting off to sleep, remembering the one night Evvie and I had spent together, my last one before shipping out, remembering the sensations of her curled up against me, I thought I heard a rustling noise outside the house. It could have been my imagination or the wind. I waited. Another minute passed. Surely it was just my exhausted body playing tricks on my restless brain.

"The shoji screen door slid open.

"I peered through the darkness. A soldier was silhouetted in the doorway against the star-studded sky, a knife in his hand. Another soldier stood behind him carrying a rifle.

"Holding my breath, I observed the one in the lead cross the room and stand over Kuniko. He nudged her awake with his foot, flashed the knife and told her not to make a sound. Instinctively she grasped her husband's shoulder. Seki awoke with a groggy jolt, saw the invader and made a move toward him. The soldier growled at him, told him to be still or his comrade would shoot him and the old woman, who was snoring only a couple of feet away. He crouched beside Kuniko and pressed the knife to her throat. She froze and whimpered.

"The old woman snorted, opened her eyes, processed what was going on and began to scream. The soldier backhanded her so hard she slammed against the wall, where she lay moaning in a semiconscious stupor.

"There was a full moon that night. Maybe because so much light was spilling in through the open doorway, my corner was obliterated in darkness. The rifleman stood sentry outside on the doorsill. I remained completely still.

"The knife bearer ordered Kuniko to open her kimono. Terrified, she eyed him, then her husband. Helpless, humiliated in his own home, Seki peered over to where I was. I put a finger to my lips and, staying in the shadows, edged toward the doorway.

"Over his shoulder the inside man instructed his cohort to shoot Seki and the old woman if either of them tried to interfere. Not likely, I calculated, since the sound of gunfire would bring unwelcome company, but I didn't suppose his victims had figured that out yet. They were too terrified.

"Clearly neither of the intruders was aware of my presence. The would-be rapist placed his knife on the tatami floor at the foot of Kuniko's futon, stood up, again commanded her to open her kimono and began to unbutton his pants.

"While he had his back to me, I leaped, grabbed the rifle barrel protruding inside the doorway, prayed to God he didn't pull the trigger and rammed the butt as hard as I could into the man's groin. As he doubled over, I brought my knee up and smashed it into his face. He tumbled backward, I sprang over to the knife on the floor, snatched it up, flew back and buried it in the rifleman's neck. He made gurgling sounds as he staggered back and collapsed onto the outside stone step.

"I spun around. Seki, not nearly as fast or limber as I, had thrown himself over his wife to protect her from the would-be rapist. It had taken me only seconds to dispatch the soldier's cohort. In that tiny interval, he'd gotten his mind off his private parts, stopped fumbling with his pants and was blindly searching on the floor for the knife that wasn't there. I dived across the room and tackled him. Lithe and quick, he squirmed out from under me and established distance. The two of us danced around each other, neither of us able to get a grip on the other.

"Then it struck me. Inspiration. My secret weapon.

"'Come and get me, you cowardly little dung beetle,' I snapped out in colloquial Japanese.

"The distraction momentarily froze him. I leaped. Within two heartbeats I had my hands around his neck and was lifting him off the floor. As I squeezed, I could see his face in the silver moonlight begin to darken. His arms flailed. His hands tried to claw me. Guttural sounds emanated from his throat. I continued to apply crushing pressure. His eyes bulged, pleaded, began to grow dim, distant. Dead. His body sagged. He went limp. Still I didn't release him—until I felt something in his neck snap.

"I let go. His body tumbled to the floor like a skein of soggy soba noodles.

"In a matter of a minute and a half, I had killed two men, one with my bare hands. I had stared into the face of the second man, watched the life seep out of his eyes, felt it drain from his body. More than sixty years have gone by. How many thousands of days and nights is that? Yet whenever I close my eyes I can still see his face. I can still feel his pulse beneath my fingers slowing, stopping."

Chapter 23

Edgar continued, "It was dawn by the time Seki and I finished disposing of the bodies, burying them in the sand along the beach, practically under the eyes of a roving patrol, and retreated to the house. By then the women had cleaned up the bloody mess by the doorway and prepared our meager breakfast.

"That morning Kuniko offered me her portion of rice, which presented me with a dilemma. To refuse it would have been an insult. To accept would have meant her going hungry. I finally compromised by accepting one meager mouthful and handing the bowl back to her with my humble request that she finish it for me.

"Seki, Kuniko and I plodded out to the fields for

another day of grueling labor, while Grandma, the side of her face black and blue, tended to household duties. We kept waiting for someone to show up and arrest us, perhaps shoot us all on the spot, but no one ever did.

"The months dragged on. Food became still more scarce, and I wondered how much longer any of us could survive.

"From radio reports we were aware that U.S. planes had been hitting targets on Honshu, the main island where Tokyo was located. Yokohama, their major seaport, was under nearly daily attack. Military and civilian casualties were mounting. Still there was no discussion of surrender. The general staff insisted Japan would remain faithful to the warrior traditions of bushido and the samurai. In other words, she would go down in flames, but she would never give up.

"Then, one day we heard about a really big bomb hitting a coastal city on Honshu called Hiroshima. The reports seemed wildly exaggerated. One single bomb couldn't possibly destroy an entire city and kill more than fifty thousand people. I didn't know what to make of it, but obviously something important had happened.

"Three days went by and we heard of another monster bomb hitting the ancient imperial capital of Nagasaki, which was on Kyushu, where we were. Reports of dead were too fantastic to be believed.

"Two days later military trucks drove through the countryside, blaring orders for everyone to return to their houses immediately for an important announcement.

"We all listened to Seki's small crystal radio. The announcer came on and explained that Hirohito, the emperor of Japan, was about to speak to the entire nation.

"I was well aware he had only ceremonial power, but his moral authority was said to be absolute, because the people venerated him as a direct descendant of the sun god. Seki became more jittery than the night we'd buried the two soldiers. The emperor, he explained, had never spoken directly to the people. This was a historic event.

"Seki, his wife and mother sucked air between their teeth and bowed to the radio as if it were an altar.

"Two things immediately struck me when the great man himself spoke. First, that his voice was so high and thin. I'd expected the deep booming voice of a deity. The second was that I couldn't understand a word he was saying, though my comprehension of the language at this point was extensive. A narrator interrupted from time to time and repeated in ordinary Japanese what the emperor was saying. It seemed divine rulers had their own ancient lingo. Like the pope speaking Latin, I guess.

"The upshot was that he had requested the general staff to accept the American offer of unconditional surrender. He further asked that the people receive their occupiers with the dignity and courtesy befitting honorable Japanese.

"The war was over.

"I sat there on my haunches, stunned.

"The war was over. I was going home. I was going home to Evvie.

"The following morning a Japanese half truck

arrived to pick up me and the other Americans who'd been indentured as laborers.

"Saying goodbye to Seki, his wife and mother was one of the most difficult things I've ever had to do. In the months I'd lived and worked with them, we had truly become family. As the truck took me away and I looked back, I knew I'd probably never see them again. In fact I never did."

In the silence that followed, a Regulator clock, the kind that could be found in every rural railroad waiting room a century earlier, chimed four o'clock.

"We've been here nearly two hours," Edgar said, amazed at the passage of time.

They got up from the table, Edgar left a generous tip and waved goodbye to the waitress.

"Let's go to the Cactus," he suggested, when they were outside.

A block north, the old Cactus Hotel, fourteen stories high, towered over the city. Built in 1929, it had been the fourth Hilton and a landmark visible from miles away back in the days when the neon sign on the Spanish-tile hip roof was lighted. Fire regulations had forced it to shut down as a hotel more than thirty years ago. Only a few floors were being used now as office space by local businesses.

The autumn sun was dipping low in the sky, casting long shadows. The temperature had dropped a few degrees.

They headed up Oakes Street. Bram had always enjoyed his grandfather's company, but he'd never felt closer to the old man than he did today. His only regret was not asking questions earlier. No doubt his grandfather had plenty more tales to tell.

"Don't stop now, Gramps, please."

"Work had ceased at the coal mine, and the nearly five hundred prisoners in the camp were milling about idly. Rumors were flying. The war was over. It wasn't. We were about to be liberated. The guards were preparing to line us all up and shoot us.

"I went to our senior officer, an American lieutenant colonel, and explained to him what I'd heard the afternoon before.

"Acting as his interpreter, I requested an interview with the camp commandant. The guard I approached gaped at me as if I had two heads. He'd never heard an American speak Japanese the way I did.

"When we were finally escorted into the major's presence, he was sitting behind a desk that seemed too big for him.

"'I understand you are fluent in Japanese,' he said before I had a chance to address him. I bowed politely and admitted it. He shook his head as if it were the last straw.

"I retrieved an upholstered chair from against a wall and positioned it directly in front of the major's desk for my colonel, and placed a smaller stiff-backed wooden chair beside him for me. Protocol. Decorum. We were all half-starved, but we still minded our manners.

"I told the commandant I had heard the emperor the previous night, and I knew the military forces of the Empire of Japan had offered their unconditional surrender to the Americans, that the war was over. I asked what he was prepared to do to guarantee our safety and welfare until allied forces arrived to liberate us.

"The major replied that he had received no instruction in the matter, but he would forward any requests we had to his superiors.

"'Demands, not requests,' the colonel corrected him. 'We need more food and medical supplies. Now.'

"The major shrugged fatalistically and explained that he had very little food in stock for his men or for us, that we had gotten all the medical attention he was able to furnish.

"'Our government will look favorably on your humane treatment of our personnel,' I stated very formally. In other words, 'Do whatever you have to do, but get it. Immediately.'

"He nodded. He was no longer in power, and thankfully he was wise enough to realize resistance at this point would only make matters worse. I had to grant the man grudging respect. He was adaptable, as the entire nation proved to be in the months and years to come.

"It was more than two weeks before American forces finally showed up. Our liberators gave us the once-over, skinny and mangy, and were ready to wreak vengeance on our guards, but I and a few others persuaded them to check out the condition of the local population, as well as the military forces holding us. They were as bad off as we were.

"After three days of decent food, medical exams and filling out postcards to be sent to our next of kin, informing them we were alive and on our way home, we boarded a ship and set course for America. We were going home."

"The waiting and uncertainty in those last two years of the war must have been torture," Sarah said.

"For me and for millions of others. I believe the Chinese have an ancient curse that wishes you live in interesting times. Those were definitely interesting times. Busy, too.

"My little cousin Benjy started first grade in 1944. His sister, Joan, went into kindergarten the following year. As I watched them go off to school in the morning, I couldn't help thinking of Henry and me doing the same thing at their ages. Mom continued to take in laundry, while I worked at the airfield during the day, sewed at night and tended our victory garden on weekends.

"I had no one to write letters to now, so I started keeping a diary, often in the form of letters to Edgar, even to my dead brother. I can imagine what the shrinks would say about that."

"That it was good therapy," Sarah replied. "You still miss him, don't you?"

"Henry's been gone more than sixty years now, and, yes, I still miss my big brother. He was so young when he died, and yet in my mind he's aged right along with me. It's weird. I picture him as bald now, but he hasn't lost that impish smile."

Evvie sagged against the back of her chair, veiny hands dangling over the armrests. Her still-vibrant emerald-green eyes assumed a faraway expression for a few seconds, then she snapped herself out of it and continued her narrative.

"On May 8, 1945, the war in Europe ended. It was such a happy time. So many families in San Angelo had men over there. The entire town seemed possessed by a feeling of jubilation, one I should have shared but couldn't. Henry wasn't coming home. My beloved brother was never coming home. And what about Edgar? Was he dead, too?

"MacArthur had returned triumphant to the Philippines, but the war in the Pacific dragged on. Casualty reports from the battle to seize the island of Okinawa were mind-boggling. Everyone was saying the invasion of Japan itself was imminent and that the losses on both sides would be astronomical, as many as a million people, military and civilian. Why didn't the damn Japanese just give up? I raged. What was the point of fighting on when it was obvious they couldn't win?

"With the Nazis defeated, there was talk now of transferring military units from Europe to the Pacific for the invasion and occupation of the Japanese home islands. The killing would continue. More people would die.

"One day early in August we heard on the radio we'd dropped an atomic bomb on Japan, a bomb so huge it was the equivalent of thousands and thousands of tons of TNT. I didn't fully understand what that meant, except it was big and it meant the Japanese were doomed.

"Still, they didn't sue for peace. Three days later we dropped another atomic bomb on them. Over a hundred thousand Japanese were reported to have died in the two raids. All anyone wanted now was for the dying and killing to stop. We wanted peace.

"This time reason won out and the Japanese capitulated. It would take several more weeks for the paperwork to be signed, but the war was finally over.

"I waited for word of Edgar. Was he alive? Had he been captured? Was he wounded? Crippled? I'd accept him any way I could get him. All I wanted was to have him back."

Chapter 24

"The journey home was more tense than you might have expected," Edgar told Bram. "The fighting had ended, so of course there was an atmosphere of relief and jubilation. We didn't have to worry about being attacked by Zeros or torpedoed by subs—at least, we hoped we didn't. We couldn't be sure if all the Imperial forces had gotten the word or if they would honor it. Most of our thoughts, though, were on other concerns.

"What would we find at home? There were fellas on board ship who'd been badly wounded, maimed for life. Those of us who hadn't been injured had still been changed. We'd lost our innocence. How would the people back home receive us?

"Now that I was in safe hands, I suddenly became too weak to walk. I'd been able to stride into the camp commandant's office and voice our senior officer's demands, but now I had trouble standing on my own two legs. I felt like a fool, a wimp.

"The medico laughed. 'You've been running on empty for a long time, Lieutenant. Well, you just ran out of fumes. Don't worry, son. Before long you'll be dancing with your best girl and getting slapped for putting your hands where they don't belong.'

"My best girl. My only girl. I thought about Evvie, dreamed about Evvie. Would she even recognize me? I'd caught a glimpse of myself in a mirror and been shocked at what I'd seen. Icabod Crane could have passed for Tarzan compared with me.

"I wrote her a letter on the cruise to Hawaii. I was going to call her from there—damn the cost. I had more than two years of back pay coming, so I would be flush, but when we anchored in Pearl it was only long enough to refuel. A few guys wrangled a couple of hours' shore leave, but I wasn't one of them. As much as I wanted to make that phone call, I didn't have the strength to even walk the gangway to the dock. I learned later getting a line to the States was nigh on impossible anyway.

"We shoved off again, this time bound for Long Beach, California, just down from L.A. I remembered Evvie telling me how much her brother had liked California. My parents and I had gone through San Francisco back in the early thirties on our way to China. I remembered loving the quaint, hilly city even then. When we returned nearly ten years later, they'd built the Golden Gate Bridge. I'd gazed in awe at it, glowing in the late-afternoon sun. Definitely a place where I wouldn't mind living, but I wasn't sure if Evvie would. Its associations with her brother might be too much. Still, I'd never seen the southern part of the state. Would I have time to play tourist?

"I didn't, but an event transpired at the port that shook me badly.

"Out of my original crew of nine, only four of us had survived. One was Sparky, the radio operator I told you about. His real name was Martin, but nobody ever called him that.

"Remarkably he still had his fiancée's picture. On the voyage from Hawaii he proudly showed it to me. It was so tattered, creased and faded I could barely make out the image, but it was enough for him to see the beautiful girl he'd left behind.

"We were together when we disembarked at Long Beach. I was scheduled to catch a train for the rest of my journey to West Texas. Like me, Sparky had sent a postcard ahead, telling Patsy he was coming home.

"She had taken the train down from San Jose and was at the dock to meet him. I watched them hug, heard her welcome him back safely, but after a moment I detected apprehension rather than relief in her eyes.

"He babbled on, asked her a barrage of questions. She fumbled with answers and finally broke down in tears. He tried to assure her he was perfectly fine, that he'd sustained no permanent injuries. The war was over. They could get on with their lives now.

"'They told me you were dead,' she said.

"He laughed. 'I felt that way a few times, but as you can see, I'm not.'

"Then she told him she had married someone else.

"He stared at her. 'You couldn't have. It's not true,' he mumbled. He glanced down at her left hand and the wedding ring on her finger. 'You promised me—'

"'I thought you were dead,' she repeated.

"The look of abject misery on Sparky's face was heartbreaking. She'd been the inspiration for him to endure years of pure hell because he loved her and was sure she was waiting for him, and she'd married someone else.

"'Why did you even bother showing up here?' he demanded. 'Why didn't you just stay away?'

"She couldn't meet his eyes. 'I should have. Part of me wanted to. Everybody said I should, but I couldn't. I had to tell you myself. I'm sorry, Marty.' She was sobbing now, tears streaming down her face. 'I'm so sorry.'

"'Leave him,' he snapped. 'Tell him it was a mistake, that I'm back now. You love me. Me. I love you, Patsy. I thought only about you.' His cheeks were wet, too. 'Tell him—'

"She shook her head, her face awash with fresh tears. 'I can't, Marty. We…we have a baby, a little boy. He's only a year old. Dan is a wonderful father, a good husband. I love him.'

"They were still crying when I made my way to the

troop train a little while later. Poor sap. Tough break. All those nights when Sparky had talked about her, about what they would do when he got home, about the children they would have together, and here she had gone and started a family with another man.

"I'd planned to call Evvie from the train station, but by the time I got there all the phone booths were busy, and my train was about to leave. The call would have to wait.

"I slept most of the way through Arizona and New Mexico. My waking moments felt more like nightmares as I debated with myself. Patsy had been told Sparky was dead. Had Evvie been told I was, too? Patsy had found someone else. Had Evvie? After all, I had been missing almost three years. Was she still at Miss Hattie's? Except for that one money order, I'd never been able to send her the money I'd promised. Maybe she'd met a wealthy patron who could afford to give her a better life.

"Then I'd remember Mei Lin and a wave of guilt would overwhelm me. What right did I have to judge Evvie when I'd slept with another woman? I had no excuse for my unfaithfulness.

"Whether it was a relapse from the dysentery I'd suffered in Japan or something I ate on the train, I can't say, but I was bushwhacked by another case of the trots about the time we crossed the Texas border. A heavy dose of Kaopectate finally got it under control, but it left me feeling like a wet dishrag and with about as much energy. Flat on my back on a stretcher wasn't the way I'd envisioned being reunited with Evvie, but when we clanged to a halt at the San Angelo train station, I was still too weak to walk.

"There was a crowd gathered to meet us at the station. I searched it, checked every female face. Evvie wasn't among them. My morale plummeted. I'd sent her a card from Japan, telling her I was alive and well and on my way back to the States. I hadn't been able to tell her exactly when I'd be arriving in San Angelo, because I hadn't known. No reason she should appear at the railroad station every time a train chugged in, I told myself. Except, all these other people had shown up.

"Maybe, unlike Patsy, Evvie didn't have the courage to meet me face-to-face and tell me she had married someone else."

"I was sitting at my desk in the supply room, processing requisitions, adding them to the mound of papers I had to file, when I saw the white ambulance bus pull up in front of the hospital across the street. More G.I.s being brought in for their final stages of treatment before being released. On stretchers. Using crutches. A few ambulatory enough to walk under their own power or leaning on corpsmen.

"'They look like cadavers,' I said to Wes, my supervisor. 'They're so emaciated.'

"'Japanese POWs,' he said sympathetically. 'My wife heard about them coming in from one of the women volunteers at mah-jongg last night.'

"I decided to take my lunch break early that day, so I could go over and visit with the latest arrivals. Maybe one of them would have news of Edgar. Suppose they confirmed he was dead?

"No private rooms in those days. Open wards. A wide aisle between two long rows of beds. I started at one end and spent a few minutes with each of the newcomers who were awake. The atmosphere was different from a year ago when the war was still raging. These guys knew it was over, not just for them but for everybody, and they didn't carry the burden of guilt so many of their predecessors had about letting their buddies down by getting wounded.

"I made my usual offer to write letters and phone people collect.

"Since these G.I.s had all served in the Pacific theater, I asked each of them if they were acquainted with Lieutenant Edgar Clyburn. None was. I was disappointed but not surprised. There were millions of men in uniform in hundreds of different outfits.

"I was about three-quarters of the way down the right side of the room when I glanced over at the man in the last bed. He'd been sleeping when I arrived, his face averted. Just then he woke up, turned his head. Our eyes met. He smiled.

"And the world stopped on its axis.

"Edgar.

"My knees turned to water. My hands flew to my mouth. Tears began to stream down my face. I didn't say a word. Just stared. He continued to smile at me and the rest of the room disappeared.

"I flew to him, hugged him, kissed him, hugged him some more, cried, searched for words, made incoherent sounds and kissed him repeatedly. His hands. His cheeks. His lips.

"The room exploded in whoops and catcalls. I laughed through my tears, unable to keep myself from kissing him yet again.

"As I gazed at him, I realized that, had he not smiled, I might never have recognized him. His cheeks were hollow. His temples indented. I could see purple veins throbbing there. His blue eyes were sunken. Lips thin, chapped, papery. His hair was buzz-cut, but it seemed to me there was gray in it. His hands appeared too large for his bony wrists. His shoulders were still wide, but angular now, rather than massive. The chest that had been so brawny and powerful seemed flat, almost concave.

"Dear God, what had they done to him?

"At last I found my voice and started asking questions.

"'Are you all right?'

"'I have all my body parts, if that's what you mean.'

"*This is no joking matter,* I wanted to shout.

"'But are you all right?' I repeated.

"'A little tired. Or I was. Not anymore.' He smiled and my heart skipped another beat, several beats.

"'Why didn't you let me know you were alive, safe, that you were coming home?'

"'I did,' he insisted. 'I sent you a card right after we were liberated. Didn't you receive it?'

"I shook my head.

"There was something in his eyes, something indefinable I didn't remember being there before. This wasn't the teenager I'd met in the parlor of Miss

Hattie's, Panama hat in hand, or even the young soldier I'd said goodbye to less than a year later. This man was aged. I don't mean in the physical sense, but in the depths of his eyes. I discovered life weariness there. Well, why not, after all he'd obviously been through? Except I thought I detected remorse, as well. But that didn't make sense. He was a survivor. A hero. Or was he more seriously injured than he was telling me? Was he dying? I needed to check his chart.

"'God, you're beautiful, Evvie. You're so beautiful.'

"Fresh tears blurred my vision.

"He squeezed my hand almost painfully. That was when I noticed his eyes were watering, too. Edgar was crying. My big, strong protector, the man I adored, the man I loved, was crying. I'd never seen him cry before.

"'I thought about you every day, Evvie. I dreamed about you every night. If it hadn't been for you, I don't think I could have made it.'

"'Shh. You're home now,' I said. 'You're safe. Everything is going to be fine. The people here will have you up and on your feet in no time.'

"'Oh, I'm okay, really,' he assured me, pulling himself together. 'A little weak at the moment, but that'll pass. A few decent meals—'

"I laughed. 'Nobody ever calls hospital food decent, Edgar, but—'

"He clutched my hand, almost desperately. 'How are you, Evvie? Really. I promised to send you money every month. I wanted to. I started to, but…' Then he looked at me anxiously. 'Are you still at Miss Hattie's?'

"'What?'

"'I wanted so much to send you the money so you could leave. If you're still at—'

"I gaped at him.

"''Cause if you are still working, there—'

"*My God,* I thought, *he thinks I'm still a whore.* 'I—'

"''Cause if you are—'

"I jerked back, jumped to my feet and tried to wipe the tears from my face with the back of a shaky hand. Still weeping, I whirled and bolted out of the room.

"'Evvie?' He called after me several times, but I kept running. 'Evvie, come back!'"

Chapter 25

"**I** stormed back to the office and commenced to slam things around," Evvie continued. "I was so ashamed, so miserably disappointed and hurt. I cried at my desk, even got the paperwork all wet with my tears.

"My boss asked me what was wrong. I told him it was none of his damn business. He gave me the eye, then got up and left the office.

"Twenty minutes later when he returned, I told him I was sorry, that it wouldn't happen again.

"He accepted my apology but this time didn't ask me what the problem was, which made me feel even worse. Wes was a good guy. He had a twenty-two-year-old son in the Marine Corps who'd been wounded at

Iwo Jima and was recovering at a naval hospital on the West Coast. Wes had enough on his plate, worrying about him without getting lip from me.

"Why don't you take off for the rest of the afternoon," he suggested. "Obviously you're not going to be worth a damn around here." He said it in a joking way, trying to lighten the moment. "I'll consider it compensatory time off for the extra work you did last week when we got that shipment of aircraft parts in."

"I hadn't worked overtime in more than a month, but I wasn't about to argue with him. I'd make the time up later.

"Mom showed instant alarm when I walked into the kitchen at one o'clock in the afternoon. She was ironing tan uniform shirts, which required precise pleats front and back. She placed the hot iron on its metal stand and wanted to know what was wrong. I didn't tell her to mind her own business. I vented.

"Her face lit up, her watery eyes sparkled, when I told her Edgar was back. She turned off the low gas flame she'd had going under an old flat iron and poured us both cups of coffee from the percolator she kept on the back of the stove.

"How was he? she asked. How badly had he been hurt? Was he going to recover completely and how soon?

"I felt like the worst person in the world when I realized I didn't have precise answers for her. He was whole, skinny and weak, I told her. Beyond that I couldn't say. I'd been so upset about his question I'd forgotten to check his chart or quiz the head nurse about him.

"Tears rolled down my face. My Edgar.

"Go lie down," Mom said. "I've got some shopping to do. The kids are going over to Mrs. Shilling's after school, so they won't bother you. Take a nap. You'll feel better."

"She went to the oatmeal box and removed several bills. "I'll be back in a couple of hours and start supper."

"I nodded, poured the rest of the tepid coffee from the nearly empty pot into the heavy china mug and sat on the back porch, sipping the brackish sludge. I scanned the summer-scorched back lawn, the green spot that was our little victory garden—it would be time to harvest the turnips and beets pretty soon—then went inside and curled up on the couch.

"What was I going to do? What was I ever going to do?

"I'd been waiting for Edgar to come home for over three years, praying for him, dreaming about him. Now he'd returned. He was safe. I longed to hold him, to nurse him, to help him regain his strength. I'd let him tell me about what he'd gone through, if he wanted to. Most guys didn't, and I wouldn't push. I'd heard enough accounts to know what men endured in combat changed them. Changed them forever.

"I pictured him in the hospital bed. He'd said he had all his body parts. He clearly had no limbs missing. He had all his fingers and presumably all his toes. He seemed able to move them without difficulty. He wasn't blind or deaf. His hair had thinned, but the hairline hadn't receded. It would grow back. Not that it mattered. I'd never loved him for his hair. I'd loved the man. I still did. I always would.

"When he went away, he'd said he loved me, but he couldn't love me now. I'd never be good enough for him, not after all he had gone through. I had no right even to think he would desire me again.

"He was still handsome, though, and I could still lose myself in his incredible blue eyes. His smile still made me smile, too.

"But suppose there was something wrong with him he hadn't told me about. He'd been a prisoner in a POW camp. He must have suffered terribly. Instead of just being tired as he said, suppose he was dying. Rather than focus on him, I'd been worried about myself. I felt so ashamed. He must despise me. He'd posed only one question—whether I was still turning tricks at Miss Hattie's.

"Why didn't I just say no?

"Because it didn't matter.

"Because Rosie had been right. Once a whore, always a whore.

"Edgar had come back a different man, but I was still a whore. I would always be a whore.

"I would have died rather than go back to that life, to the degradation, the humiliation. But like the G.I.s who returned home irreparably damaged, I could never go back to who and what I had been before I climbed the wooden stairs in the alley behind number eighteen and a half.

"My heart ached.

"There was only one thing left for me to do. Walk away. Leave him free to be the man he was, the person he could become."

"I would have gotten up and punched something or someone after Evvie ran out if I'd had the strength," Edgar said. "I couldn't believe how weak and tired I felt, so debilitated that at times I wondered if there might be more wrong with me than just malnutrition and the aftereffects of dysentery, something the docs hadn't been willing to tell me.

"My question to Evvie had probably been a bit abrupt, a little insensitive, I realized, but the answer was also very obvious. She was still working at Miss Hattie's. Otherwise she would have simply told me no. I was so disheartened. I'd promised to send her money to get out of that place, and I hadn't. Well, I hadn't had a chance to, damn it. For a moment my mind flashed to Mei Lin, and I wondered how she was. I had no doubt after I was shot down she went back to working at the House of the Eight Immortals. For her there would never be any options.

"There were for Evvie. If only she'd let me...

"God, she looked good, as sweet as I remembered her, and even more beautiful. The feel of her lips when she kissed me. The scent of her soft skin when she hugged me. Oh, yes, I was still a man, I reflected with considerable satisfaction as I lay there and felt myself react to the recollection of her touch and taste and smell.

"How I yearned for her. How I ached to hold her in my arms, stretch out beside her, explore and treasure every nuance of her being. How I longed to gaze into her mesmerizing jade eyes and lose myself in the love I beheld reflected there.

"But of course she didn't know me anymore. She didn't realize I'd been unfaithful to her, or that I'd stabbed one man to death, then strangled another while I watched the light fade from his eyes.

"I'd had no choice. Kill or be killed. Kill or witness three people humiliated, disgraced and in the end probably murdered, as well.

"I had no such excuse with Mei Lin. I had willfully and selfishly chosen to sleep with another woman, when I owed my honor and my fidelity to Evvie, to the woman I loved.

"I caught movement out of the corner of my eye, shifted my head and smiled at the sight of Evvie's mother coming down the aisle toward me, a white box in her hands.

"Wilma's eyes were moist as she stood at the foot of my bed, appraising me, trying to smile. Her hands shook as she placed the bakery box on the bedside table, then she threw her arms across my shoulders and gave me a great big hug.

"'Welcome home,' she murmured, brushing away tears.

"I, too, felt tears well up. I reflected on Henry, the son who would never be coming home, and suddenly I felt guilty for being there.

"We held hands for a long time, quietly gazing into each other's eyes. Finally I asked the usual questions— how she was, how the children were. Fine. Fine.

"The awkwardness between us grew.

"'What's in the box?' I inquired.

"'Oh, cookies. I figured you and your friends might enjoy them.'

"Three pounds of cookies. Assorted. Tollhouse. Oatmeal-raisin. Sugar. Butter.

"'I would have baked some myself,' she said apologetically, 'but I didn't have time.'

"'Just your being here is enough.'

"'Better hide them,' the guy in the next bed warned us. His left arm was in a sling, the fingers splayed in a metal cage, and his left leg in a cast. 'Or the head nurse will confiscate them.'

"'Oh, dear,' Wilma said. 'I hadn't thought of that.'

"Evvie had inherited her mother's hair, chestnut in the sun, auburn indoors. Wilma's wasn't as shiny, and it was sprinkled with gray. She appeared older than her midforties. Worn and weary. Her life had been physically hard back in Oklahoma. Even harder emotionally here in Texas.

"'Don't worry, ma'am,' the guy in the next bed said. He smiled, exposing a couple of missing teeth. 'We'll take real good care of them.'

"'Stick them in the bottom of the bedside table,' I told her.

"First she offered me my choice from the box, then carried it down the line. Nobody who was awake passed them up. She tendered me another and tucked the nearly empty box into the lower compartment of the metal bed stand.

"She barraged me with questions. Where I had been. What had happened to me. More than Evvie had gotten around to asking.

"I gave her the abbreviated version—that I'd been stationed in China, that I'd been shot down and taken prisoner by the Japanese. Then, I don't know why, but I told her about the two men I'd killed.

"To my utter surprise she didn't pull back in shocked horror. Instead she regarded me sympathetically.

"'If you had it to do over again,' she asked, 'would you?'

"I pictured tiny, half-starved Kuniko and the terror in her eyes when the Japanese soldier stood over her, holding a knife, telling her to open her kimono. I rec-ollected the helpless humiliation on her crippled husband's face as she silently implored him for help and how a few moments later Seki had covered her with his body, prepared to take the knife in his back to protect her honor. Most of all, I reflected on how I envied those people for the love they shared, how I burned to share that kind of unconditional commit-ment with Evvie.

"'Yes,' I said without hesitation. 'I'd do it all over again.'

"She squeezed my hand. 'Then you have nothing to be ashamed of.'

"Emboldened, I started to tell her about Mei Lin, but she stopped me before I got to the salient part.

"'At some point you may want or need to tell Evvie about what happened in Japan,' she said.

"I didn't realize it at the time, but she was referring to the nightmares I would later have.

"'If I may offer a piece of advice, don't tell her anything you wouldn't want her to tell you.'

"I gaped at her, understanding immediately what she meant. Then I nodded.

"'She's mad at me,' I said a few seconds later. 'She thinks I blame her for still being at Miss Hattie's. I'd hoped—'

"Wilma smiled at me, a sad watery smile that nevertheless contained an unexpected pride. 'Oh, Edgar,' she said. 'Evvie left Miss Hattie's almost three years ago, just before you sent her the money.'

"'Before?' I asked. 'But—'

"'She'd already gotten a job here on the post. She wrote you about it. I guess you didn't get the letter. We heard shortly after that you'd been shot down.'

"Evvie had left Miss Hattie's on her own, without any help from me. I felt so proud of her. And confused.

"'But why didn't she just tell me that?'

"It was then that comprehension dawned, and why Wilma was here. My God, how could I have been so stupid, so naive, so arrogantly vain? It wasn't because of Miss Hattie that Evvie had run out. I remembered Sparky. My spirits dropped. There was an ache in my chest where my heart had been.

"'There's someone else, isn't there? She married somebody else.'

"Wilma's startled expression transformed into a gleeful grin, followed by a soft chuckle.

"'Edgar, there's only ever been one man for her, and

I think ever will be. You. There's no one else. She's spent the past three years waiting for the day you'd come home.'

"'But—'

"She rubbed my fingers. 'She's convinced you don't want her anymore—'

"'Don't want her? She's the only woman I've ever wanted. Ever. Not want her? Is she crazy?'

"Wilma laughed and her whole face lit up as I'd never seen it before. 'Don't tell *me* that, Edgar Clyburn. Tell her.'

"A nurse appeared in the doorway and announced visiting hours were over.

"This was the most personal conversation Wilma and I ever had—or ever would have."

"I'm sure I was red eyed the next morning when I arrived at the office," Evvie admitted. "I hadn't been able to sleep. I kept visualizing Edgar, the way he had been when he went away and the way he was now. I cried. Where all the tears came from I can't imagine. I cried through supper. I cried while I was doing the dishes afterward. I went to bed and cried some more.

"I slouched at my desk, lethargically sorting the forms that had accumulated the previous afternoon. I remember at one point throwing the originals away and saving the carbon papers.

"'Evvie,' my boss said.

"'What?' I snapped without bothering to look up.

"'Evvie, you have a visitor.'

"He was standing there. Edgar. Wearing a wrinkled

hospital bathrobe over an equally wrinkled hospital gown. Cloth slippers that couldn't have offered much comfort on the hot asphalt road he'd had to cross.

"Wes brought up a stiff wooden chair and placed it behind him. 'Better sit down, soldier, before you fall. I know the head nurse over there and—' he guided Edgar to the seat '—she's going to give us both hell when she finds out you're here.'

"Edgar and I continued to stare at each other.

"Wes gave us an assessing glance, shook his head good-naturedly and announced he was going to pick up distribution, shrugged at our lack of response and disappeared.

"My chest was pounding. My hands shook. Edgar was so scrawny. I ached to envelop him in my arms, hug him.

"'Edgar,' I mumbled, 'I—'

"'I have one thing to say to you—' his voice was stronger than it had been at the hospital, more determined '—and one thing to ask.'

"'I—'

"'Just be quiet and listen to me.' He sounded so serious, so stern, but then he cracked a smile, which instantly took the sting out of his words. I remembered the first time I'd ever seen him, standing at the head of the stairs, his hand still on the newel post, and how my insides had turned to Jell-O when our eyes met. My insides were turning to Jell-O again.

"'Yes, sir.'

"'What I want to tell you…' He seemed suddenly unsure of himself. 'What I want to say, Evvie, is I love you. I fell in love with you the first time I laid eyes on you. I've continued to love you, and I always will.'

"I bit my lip, grateful I was already sitting, because I felt so weak.

"'What I need to ask you,' he said quietly, 'is, will you marry me, Evvie?'

"My heart swelled, and for a moment I was actually afraid I was going to pass out. I'd waited so long to hear those words. I wanted this man more than anything I'd ever wanted in my life.

"'I…' I began, but couldn't seem to form words.

"'Evvie—' He started to get up.

"'I can't marry you, Edgar,' I blurted out, my heart thudding, shattering.

"He fell back into the chair. 'What?'

"Sobbing, I lowered my head, unable to meet his eyes. 'You know what I am, Edgar. What I was,' I corrected myself. 'It wouldn't be fair to burden you with what people will think of me.' My voice cracked. 'I can't marry you, Edgar. It wouldn't be right. You deserve better than me.'

"This time he rose and made his way around the corner of my desk and stood over me. 'It's the only thing that is right, Evvie.' Bracing a hand on the edge of the desk, he slowly, deliberately settled onto one knee beside me.

"I was flustered, worried about him hurting himself. I jumped up and tried to coax him to his feet.

"'Sit down, Evvie,' he commanded. 'We need to talk. I need to tell you things.'

"He was scaring me. He was sick and weak, and he had no business kneeling on the floor. Yet the strength in his voice, the fire in his eyes... 'Please sit down, Edgar. Please.'

"I dodged around the side of the desk and grabbed the chair he'd been sitting on and positioned it beside mine. With a chuckle that surprised me and a grunt of effort, he worked himself up onto the wooden seat. Then he took my hands into his. They were as cold as steel, but as he continued to hold mine, I could feel them warming. My heart was racing.

"'I've learned things since I've been away, sweetheart. I've learned that sometimes we have to do things we don't want to do. I've done things I wish I hadn't, things I'm not proud of, things you'd hate me for if you knew—'

"I freed one of my hands and stroked his cheek. 'I'll never hate you, Edgar. Never.'

"He paused, and I realized his eyes were glassy. 'Some of the things I've done involved choices I didn't want to make, but I couldn't see any alternatives. Oh, Evvie, I love you so much it hurts. I don't deserve your love. I'm not worthy of it, but—'

"Tears were streaming down his face. It was unnerving to behold this man, who in my mind was still big and strong and powerful, with tears staining his cheeks, yet I also felt something inside me I couldn't describe, something sweet, an overwhelming sensation of euphoria, like none I'd ever experienced. I gazed into his eyes and realized I was crying, too. I strained to tell him how much I loved him, but I couldn't get the words past the burning in my throat.

"He was fighting for control, as well. A moment passed. The two of us faced each other, holding hands, not quite smiling, tears still running down our faces.

"Finally, leaning forward, he kissed me softly on the lips. 'Please tell me you'll marry me.'

"Speech was impossible for me. All I could do was nod.

"He rose again to his feet, stronger now, it seemed to me, and extended his hands to help me up. I jumped into his arms. He was so bony, but it didn't matter.

"'I've always loved only you, Evvie,' he murmured into my ear. 'I promise to love, honor and be faithful to you for the rest of my life. Always, Evvie. Only you.'

"'I love you, Edgar,' I managed to say just before we kissed."

Chapter 26

"How long did it take you to recover?" Bram asked as they continued up Oakes Street toward Twohig.

"Not very long at all. Maybe all the world traveling I'd done with my parents had built up my immune system so I was able to ward off the fevers and parasites so many of the other prisoners fell prey to. Within a matter of weeks I was able to land a job with a local construction company."

"Doing manual labor? That soon? You're kidding."

Edgar smiled. "It's amazing what good food and plenty of loving can do for a man. In no time at all, I began getting restless. Sitting on the front porch watching the world go by, knowing you didn't have to dig ditches or plant rice, didn't have to worry about the next meal, if there would be a next meal, or take precautions against somebody bashing your head in just for the fun of it—well, it has a way of lifting a man's spirits. But after about three days I started to itch to be part of the world I saw prancing by out there.

"What better way to build myself up, I decided, than by hauling lumber and framing houses? Shoot, that was something I had experience in. Building.

"I didn't have a whole lot of strength or stamina at first, but the men I worked with were patient with me. Before long I was able to carry my full share of the load."

"So that's how you got into home building. I often wondered."

"I'd worked on all kinds of construction projects with my father in different parts of the world as far back as I could remember. While other kids were playing with Lego blocks and Lincoln Logs, I was playing with real bricks and timber. For some reason, though, I'd never given home building or civil engineering even passing consideration as occupations—until I got involved in carving those roads out of the jungle. There was wonderful satisfaction in creating something that hadn't been there before, even if it later got destroyed."

They stopped at the corner, heeded the cars rolling by and waited for the light to change.

"Even then I didn't realize I wanted to build houses until my first construction site here in town. I quickly concluded the contractor I was working for must have been one of Cousin Zeke's cronies. In for a quick buck.

In the long run quality pays, but this guy wasn't interested in the long haul. There was plenty of demand, so
I decided to set up my own company and do it right.
I hired a couple of former officers with engineering
and building experience and half a dozen noncoms. If
anyone knew how to organize, train and supervise
teams they did. I squeezed working capital from Zeke
and a loan from a local bank."

The traffic light changed. They crossed the street
and arrived at the Cactus Hotel. The shiny brass-and-
glass double doors under the semicircular metal and
milk glass awning weren't particularly ornate, but they
had an understated elegance. Bram held one of the
doors for his grandfather.

Beyond the small, marble-paneled vestibule was the
lobby, two stories high. Directly ahead a wide staircase
branched right and left to a balcony that ran along all
four sides of the lobby.

"Used to be a mural on the wall behind the staircase,"
Edgar observed. "Western theme, as I recall. Buffalo,
cattle, cowboys, windmills." He surveyed the deserted
lobby. "This was a classy joint back in the old days."

Definitely a step back in time, Bram decided as he
surveyed the high marble-topped registration desk and
a cashier's window encased in an ornate bronze grille.
Suspended from the milk glass skylighted ceiling were
four elaborate brass chandeliers. The floor beneath
their feet was a mosaic made up of tiny ceramic tiles in
an intricate geometric pattern.

He could easily picture gentlemen wearing western-cut suits, string ties, cowboy boots and white Stetsons accompanying ladies in slim, low-waisted outfits, medium-heeled, single-strap shoes and cloches and bellhops, decked out in red uniforms with brass buttons and pillbox hats, responding to the ding of a bell at the registration desk. Maybe the old hotel wasn't haunted, but there was definitely an other-world atmosphere about it.

They went up the stairs, kept right and entered the Crystal Ballroom.

"Brought your grandmother here to a dance after the war," Edgar continued. "She wore a jade-green dress that set off her eyes perfectly. Her hair…it was chestnut back then, down to her shoulders in soft, flowing waves that curled under…." He sighed. "The most beautiful woman in the room. That was still the big-band era. Wonderful music. We cut a rug that night, let me tell you. Danced every number—foxtrot, polka, jitterbug, even an occasional waltz and tango—till the musicians finally called it quits. Oh, what a night that was."

He scanned the painted medallions in the ceiling cornices. "I guess we'd better go buy that fudge, pick up the wine and be on our way. I reckon your grandmother has had enough time to say her piece."

Instead of walking back on Oakes, however, Edgar headed west on Twohig to Chadbourne Street, then south to Concho Avenue. They had to pass the jeweler that occupied the place where the dry-goods store had been. Concho pearls were on display in the window. Edgar stopped to examine them.

"Pretty, aren't they?"

Bram agreed. "Maybe I ought to buy one for Sarah."

"Can't go wrong buying a woman jewelry, my boy."

Mark Priest, the owner, came forward when they entered and greeted Bram by name. Bram introduced his grandfather.

"What do you think about your grandson running for the state senate?" Mark asked as they shook hands.

"Can't think of a better man for the job."

Bram explained he was interested in Concho pearls.

Mark led them to a display case that held an impressive array of rings, necklaces and brooches, all set with the rare freshwater pearls.

After hemming and hawing, Bram selected a necklace. A gold heart with a lavender pearl set in the center, surrounded with small diamonds.

While it was being gift wrapped, Edgar picked up a brochure from the counter advertising Miss Hattie's Bordello Museum upstairs.

"Would you like to take the tour, Mr. Clyburn?" Mark asked. "Be glad to show you around." He returned Bram's credit card.

It's been sixty-five years, the old man thought. *Do I dare go up there?*

Mark retrieved the key from under the counter and led them outside to the street entrance to number eighteen and a half.

Beyond the glass-paneled door a wide wooden staircase creaked and groaned as they mounted it. Didn't feel as solid as it had back in 1941, but the sense of anticipation Edgar experienced was just as real.

The parlor at the top was smaller than he remembered it. He surveyed the shadowy room. Not all the furniture or accessories were the same, he realized. The linoleum on the floor was original, though. It was here, sitting on this settee by the staircase, that he first saw Evvie. He could picture her, so young and fresh and innocent.

Mark ushered them into the dining room, showed them the closet-size kitchen, and the adjoining sitting room overlooking Concho Avenue. Was that the same Victrola against the far wall? Shouldn't it be in the other corner by the window? Edgar examined the rest of the room. The building was over a hundred years old now, and even though Mark was doing his best to lovingly and faithfully preserve it, its age showed.

Their host was saying something about the furniture in the various rooms as he led them toward the narrow hallway, but Edgar wasn't listening. Everything seemed slightly out of kilter, as if he were viewing the world through a distorting lens.

The desk in the first room on the right, Miss Hattie's personal parlor, was different, but he had no trouble picturing the one that had been there or the woman who'd sat at it, collecting money, dispensing tokens, scribbling notes with a dip pen in the long leather-and-cloth ledger. She hadn't been a bad person, he mused. Whatever happened to her '35 LaSalle? Be worth a fortune today. But then, so would the Packard she hadn't bought. Recollection of that unsuccessful sale made him smile. Bless Cousin Zeke for sending him here. How else would he ever have met Evvie?

Bram was asking Mark questions, but Edgar wasn't paying attention. His mind was alive with memories of a time long past, of an era that seemed nostalgically quaint and fascinating to people who hadn't had to live through it.

Would he go back if he could? To feel that young again? Definitely. To meet Evvie for the first time and fall in love with her all over again? Without a doubt.

They passed by Miss Rosie's room and Goldie's, and finally arrived at the one that had been assigned to Evvie.

My God, the iron bed was still there. The chifforobe, too, its door still warped. The small, marble-topped nightstand. The chairs where they piled their clothes. He'd made love to Evvie on that bed. He conjured up that first time, the feel of her body under his. He closed his eyes...

"You all right, Gramps?"

Edgar's eyes sprang open. Both men were staring at him strangely.

"Fine, fine," he said, embarrassed by his momentary lapse.

How could he tell him he'd just been transported back in time, that for a few precious moments he'd been nineteen?

"Do you need to sit down, Mr. Clyburn?" Mark asked.

Edgar chuckled. "No, no, I'm fine," he repeated. *Just reliving memories and feeling young again.*

He and his grandson left the building a few minutes later and walked to the corner.

"Up there," Bram began a little tentatively, "you seemed to space out for a second."

The old man gave his grandson a sidelong glance. Oh, to recapture youth. "It was her room, son. Faded now, but it hasn't really changed."

They crossed the street to Eggemeyer's General Store and purchased a pound each of pecan fudge and divinity.

Next stop: to buy a good Merlot to warm the palate.

"Did Sparky ever get over Patsy?" Bram pulled out of the parking lot and proceeded west on Concho Avenue.

Edgar frowned. "He went into a deep depression for several years. Drank too much. Had a hard time holding on to jobs. But eventually he bounced back, joined AA, entered a seminary and became an ordained minister. Married a few years later and had three kids. His older son became a prominent surgeon in the Midwest somewhere, his daughter a flower child and war protester during Vietnam. Later joined the faculty at the University of Berkeley as a professor of women's studies or some such. His younger son…had a lot of issues. Turned to drugs and died of AIDS when he was twenty-four."

"So it wasn't happily ever after for him?"

"Unfortunately not. Marty died of leukemia about twenty years ago. Too young. From what I could gather, the marriage hadn't been a very happy one. Because of his war experiences? Or because he hadn't married Patsy? We'll never know. Makes me all the more grateful for Evvie and the blessings I've received."

Chapter 27

Evvie poured more tea from the pink-on-white floral pot she'd bought in a little shop outside London on one of her trips with Edgar.

"Two days after he returned to San Angelo," she told Sarah, "I got the postcard he'd sent from Japan, announcing he was alive and coming home."

Sarah chuckled. "Great timing."

"It had languished down in San Antonio for over a month before somebody noticed it said San Angelo instead of San Antonio. Not an uncommon mistake in the days before zip codes."

"How long was Edgar in the hospital?"

"Officially two weeks, then he was placed on convalescent leave. The first weekend I brought him home.

Mom didn't stop feeding him the whole time he was there. Cousin Zeke stopped by and told him he could have his old job back. Edgar thanked him but declined. Zeke didn't appear surprised."

Sarah stirred a half teaspoon of sugar into her cup. "How soon before you got married?"

"A month later." Evvie relaxed against the cushion of the wrought-iron chair. "Zeke offered us one of his better rental houses, which we did accept, especially since he let us have the first six months rent free as a homecoming and wedding present. Nothing fancy, but it was adequate. Considering housing was at a premium, we were lucky to get it. The best part was that it was only a block from Mom. I had my first baby, Bram's father, Hank—named after my brother—there less than a year later."

Sarah smiled. "Sounds like Edgar recovered fine."

"He said we had a lot of catching up to do. We had six children over the next ten years. Buried one of them." She said the last more quietly but didn't dwell on it. "We've been married over sixty years now. Our five kids have given us fourteen grandkids, and we have three great-grandkids. Not too bad for an old hooker, huh?"

Sarah cringed. "Surely you don't still think of yourself that way."

Evvie smiled and shook her head. "No, my dear, I think of myself as a very, very lucky woman."

"If you had it to do over again, would you?"

"You mean go to Miss Hattie's?" Evvie sighed. "You

have no idea how many times I've asked myself that question." She paused. "If I had to go back and make the decision again, not knowing any more than I did then, I think I'd have to do the same thing. Good can come out of bad. I found the man of my dreams and married him. He's still the man of my dreams."

She idly stirred her tea, sipped, replaced the cup on the saucer and peered at the younger woman. "Okay, enough about me. Let's talk about you."

Sarah stiffened slightly and hung her head.

"You made a mistake, my dear, but that part of your life is over. I'm not telling you it won't sneak back to haunt you occasionally. Senator Spicer's wife has made that abundantly clear. But it seems to me you have two choices—remain a prisoner of your mistake or move on."

She reached across the table and rested her hand on the young woman's.

"Bram loves you, Sarah. That's easy to see. And it's plain you love him. Otherwise the two of you wouldn't have come out here together today, clinging to each other like a couple of frightened children—" she smiled sympathetically "—and you wouldn't be willing to leave him for his own good. But if you do that, you're throwing his love away. Please don't. Don't underestimate the power of love."

Sarah gazed off into space, her eyes glassy, her lips pinched between her teeth.

"Bram has accepted you the way you are," the old woman continued, "with his eyes wide open. The reason I've told you all this is I want you to understand that what you've done isn't the end of the world."

"But you did what you had to do, out of generosity for others. What I did was out of greed and selfishness. It's not the same."

"That may be true, but let me tell you something, my dear. When a woman sells herself, nobody cares about her motivation. The important thing is Bram has forgiven you. Now it's time for you to forgive yourself."

"I don't want to hold him back, Evvie. That wouldn't be fair to him."

"Then don't. Trust him to have the strength and wisdom to take on the world for the woman he loves. That's what men do. Protect. Defend. It's one of the reasons we love them. He's aware of what the stakes are if he decides to run for office. On the other hand, if you really don't want him to go into politics, tell him. He loves you, my dear. He'll respect your wishes, and that'll give you all the more reason for loving him."

"You said earlier that sacrifice only makes more victims."

So she had been listening. "It does if the sacrifice is one-sided. Joy arises from mutual sacrifice—as long as it's completely informed and entirely voluntary. It can't be negotiated. It's quite different from compromise. What I'm trying to say is you have to trust each other to make the right decisions for both of you. I have absolute trust in Edgar, and I've never regretted putting my happiness in his care. Does that mean he's always made the right decision—or that I have? Of course not, but absolute confidence in each other's love has made it possible for us to correct our mistakes without recrimination and to love each other all the more for the shared effort."

Sarah said nothing for the moment, then asked, "Did your background ever become an issue in your marriage?"

"In our marriage? Never. Socially? It did once or twice many years ago. It's a cliché, but we found honesty to be the best policy. In the process one or two people broke off with us, but good riddance. They weren't friends after all."

Bram turned off Bryan Boulevard onto Knickerbocker Road. "What ever happened to Cousin Zeke?"

"Died in a nursing home, penniless, at the age of eighty," Edgar said. "His wife had passed away twenty years earlier. Cirrhosis of the liver."

"It sounds like he was quite a character. I'm sorry I never met him."

Edgar tilted his head to the side. "He was a contradiction in so many ways. He could be absolutely charming and completely ruthless. He loan sharked, yet he was also genuinely generous. For instance, he sent my folks money regularly at their various missions around the world, though I doubt he'd voluntarily been inside a church since he was christened as a baby. He drank too much, was unfaithful to his wife—yet I think he genuinely loved Selma. He just didn't know how to help her. He would sell plastic cookies to a starving invalid, yet he established an anonymous scholarship fund for minority high-school kids. He told me once he'd never cheated an honest man. There are a couple of ways you can interpret that, of course." Edgar snorted. "I suspect he's still in limbo while the good Lord tries to figure out what to do with him."

Bram laughed. "And your parents?"

"They stayed in Africa until the early fifties, when my father contracted one of the many exotic fevers they have over there and died three days later. Mom returned to the States, settled down here in San Angelo, not too far from us—we hadn't bought the ranch yet— and played grandma happily for the next fifteen years. She died quietly in her sleep a week after her seventieth birthday."

"Did you ever tell your parents about Grandma's background?"

"Never saw my dad after he boarded the train here on his way to the Congo, and it wasn't the type of subject I was about to put in writing. After my mother moved here, Evvie and I sat her down one afternoon and explained the situation to her, rather than take a chance on her hearing about it from someone else."

The light at University Avenue turned red, and Bram stopped behind a white pickup loaded with big bags of wood shavings. "What was her reaction?"

Edgar smiled. "Mom was a trooper. She told Evvie she was sorry she'd had such a hard life and gave her a great big hug. We never talked about it again."

"She didn't miss the missionary life?"

"To be honest I don't think she ever liked it. She

accepted it because it was her husband's calling and she truly loved him, but if she'd had her druthers, I suspect she would have been perfectly content to remain in Iowa and grow corn."

The light changed and they got under way. "And Grandma's mom?"

"Wilma was a wonderful grandmother, too, and became a second mother to me. In a way I reckon I replaced Henry for her—partially, at least. It seemed to me there was always a melancholy air about her, though, a weariness with life. She died a year after my mother, and I suspect she passed on with a sense of relief."

They arrived at the wine shop.

"Don't let me forget to pick up a bottle of Cherry Herring for your grandmother," Edgar said. "I imagine the one at home is pretty well shot by now."

Twenty minutes later, Bram finished loading the case of assorted wines and liquors his grandfather had selected, and they started back home.

"Thank you for telling me all this, Gramps. I know not all of it was easy for you."

"And some of it I've never told another living soul, but if you learned from it, son, it was worth it."

Chapter 28

By the time Bram and his grandfather arrived at the ranch house, Evvie and Sarah had made the salad—a hearty antipasto with marinated artichoke hearts, Greek olives, feta cheese and thin strips of prosciutto. Potatoes were baking in the oven, and fresh asparagus was ready to be steamed. The women were outside re-setting the glass-topped patio table.

"Since we were going to Eggemeyer's," Edgar said after giving his wife a kiss on the cheek, "we decided to stop off across the street at Legend Jewelers."

Evvie interrupted putting out place mats to regard her husband with an amused expression. "Legend Jewelers. That's at number eighteen, isn't it?"

"Uh-huh," her husband replied. "Used to be a

dry-goods store years ago. Nice place. Interesting pieces on display."

"Really?" Evvie commented, a smile playing on her lips.

Bram presented Sarah with the small black gift box. "I hope you like it."

She set down the tray containing plates, glasses and silverware on a side table and accepted the gift. "What is it?"

"Open it."

She slipped off the gold elastic band and removed the cover. Inside was a blue velvet box, which she dug out and snapped open. "Oh, Bram, how beautiful."

"A Concho pearl," Evvie said, moving closer to admire it. "They're becoming harder and harder to find. That one is really lovely."

Sarah kissed Bram on the cheek and wrapped her arms around his waist. "You didn't have to, you know."

"Maybe I did," he murmured and kissed her softly on the cheek. "I love you, Sarah."

She bowed her head as he secured the clasp behind her neck, then spread his hands reassuringly across her shoulders before releasing her. Evvie instructed her husband to light the grill for the steaks, while she brought out the first course.

"Sarah and I were looking at pictures this afternoon," Evvie said a few minutes later as they passed around the antipasto salad.

"The old album?" Edgar grinned at his wife.

"Bram, dear," Evvie said, "I left it on the sideboard

in the dining room. Would you bring it, please? There's one picture I need to point out to Sarah. You need to see it, too."

"Sure." Obediently he got up and went inside.

Edgar winked at his wife, his tongue planted firmly in his cheek.

Bram returned and stood beside his grandmother's chair. While he held the heavy volume, she flipped several pages. "There." She pointed to a snapshot from the forties. Two young women in plain below-the-knee dresses smiling into the camera.

"That's you," Sarah said, pointing to the image on the right. "Who's the other girl?"

"I mentioned that Miss Hattie never allowed herself to be photographed," Evvie said. "She also recommended we not get our pictures taken, either. Not together, at least. This is the only one I have of any of the other girls. It was snapped after I'd left Miss Hattie's, so I figured it didn't matter."

"Is this Rosie?" Sarah asked. "You said she was your best friend."

"No, this is Miss Kitty. I told you her real name was Eula Mae Fargus and that she eventually married a local rancher and settled down to raise a big family."

"Yeah, I remember."

"She never liked being called Eula. Always went by Mae." Then Evvie added, "Her married name was Spicer."

It took a moment for the information to sink in. Sarah's eyes went wide. "As in Senator Spicer?"

"His mother."

"Mae Spicer was one of Miss Hattie's girls?" Bram asked, equally astonished. He remembered the pleasant old woman.

Evvie grinned.

"I don't think you have to worry about the senator or his wife exposing skeletons in the closet, son," Edgar said. "Glass houses and all that."

"Is the senator aware of his mother's background?" Bram asked.

"Mae told him when he first entered politics," his grandmother replied. "She figured he ought to be forewarned in case it ever surfaced. It never has."

"You think Jane Spicer knows—?" Sarah began.

Evvie shook her head. "Mae's been gone ten years now, and for all his shortcomings Millard did love his mother and would do anything to protect her memory. So I doubt he told even his wife about his mother's secret past."

Edgar nodded his agreement. "I suspect the minute Jane recounted her phone call to you, Millard ordered her to drop the whole thing."

"Does *he* know about *you*, Gram?" Bram asked.

"Mae and I kept each other's secret for over forty years," Evvie responded. "She had no reason to tell him."

Bram put the album away, came back and squeezed his wife's shoulder reassuringly before sitting down. The four of them spent a leisurely hour eating and talking about horses and building projects, avoiding the main subject just as they had earlier that day at lunch. But the elephant in the room would not be ignored.

"I'm confused, folks," Bram finally said. He'd tucked away a good-size steak and now set his knife and fork squarely in the middle of his plate. "I've already said I don't want to go into politics, which makes Jane Spicer's threat to expose Sarah's background irrelevant. I agree with Gramps. If the subject ever does come up, we acknowledge it and move on."

He raised his wineglass and sipped, then turned to his grandmother.

"So, the question is why did you and Gramps even bother telling Sarah and me about you being one of Miss Hattie's girls?"

"Would you pour me a little more wine, please, dear?" Evvie's vibrant green eyes twinkled as she held up her glass.

Bram topped off hers and everyone else's. His grandmother took a sip.

"I wanted Sarah to realize that a shameful past is not insurmountable." She honed in on the younger woman.

Bram reached for his wife's hand. Biting her lip, she gave it to him.

His grandmother rotated the stem of her glass. "I worried for years about what other people would say if they found out about my past. The one person I didn't have to worry about was Edgar. Our secret didn't divide us. It brought us together. He's been my rock, the one person I've always known I could depend on."

She smiled at him, and they, too, joined hands.

"I didn't tell you about my time at Miss Hattie's," she said to Sarah, "because I'm proud of it but to demonstrate you can live with anything if you have the right man by your side."

"It's instinctive for men to protect," Edgar contributed, "and I've tried to be the guardian of my wife's peace of mind all our married life. Not because I'm ashamed of what she did. On the contrary, I'm damn proud of what this woman was willing to sacrifice to help the people she loved—her innocence for the benefit of others, without any expectation of reward, knowing full well that what she was giving up could never be returned."

"But Bram can't be proud of me like that," Sarah cried. "What Evvie did was noble and selfless. What I did was just the opposite, selfish and contemptible."

Evvie gazed at her compassionately. "And you owned up to it, my dear. You didn't try to hide it from Bram. He's accepted you for who and what you are, a flawed human being. People are. But you are also a person with love and compassion. You love him—that makes you very special to him."

"We all make mistakes," Edgar added to his grandson. "The question is how we learn from them and grow to become better individuals. This crisis is only one of many you'll encounter in your lives together, but if it results in the two of you having complete trust in each other, you'll have overcome what's probably the biggest hurdle your marriage will ever encounter."

He smiled at Sarah. "You say the two of you should

get a divorce. I'd like to know on what grounds. Because you love each other?" He snickered. "I think a judge will have a hard time with that. You're sitting here holding Bram's hand, and he's holding yours. That tells me you both want to survive this, and you can."

The young couple sat in silence for several minutes, still holding hands, gazing at each other like lovesick teenagers. Edgar was about to propose he and Evvie leave them alone—or send them to a bedroom without dessert—when she suggested they have coffee. She also announced she had cheesecake for dessert. Edgar chuckled. Not exactly what he had in mind.

"Well, maybe just a little piece," was the consensus.

Edgar patted his belly as Evvie went around a few minutes later pouring rich, hot coffee. "Good food, good wine, good company," he said. "What more could a man ask for. Besides a good wife, of course. In that regard I've been truly blessed. More than any man deserves."

"He's sucking up because he didn't buy me a pearl, too," Evvie commented.

"Did you…? I…"

Evvie laughed. "You've already bought me three, remember?" She put the carafe aside, came to Edgar, leaned over and kissed him on the temple. "I love you," she murmured, loud enough for him alone to hear.

Darkness stole in. Crickets chirped. A huge yellow moon slowly crept above the eastern horizon.

"Evvie," Sarah said, rising, "let me help you with the dishes."

"I won't hear of it, my dear. You're a guest. Besides,

I have all the help I need right here." She tilted her head and directed her thumb toward Edgar.

"In that case...Bram," Sarah said with a note of apprehension in her voice, "would you mind going for a walk with me in the garden?"

"In the moonlight? My pleasure." He climbed to his feet. "If you'll excuse us."

The two old people murmured polite replies.

Bram extended his hand. Sarah clasped it as though it were a lifeline, and the young people disappeared along the path to the rose garden.

After a short pause Evvie asked, "Did you go upstairs?"

Edgar brought her hand to his lips and kissed it. "Yes."

"What was it like?"

He took a deep breath. "Filled with ghosts."

"I almost went up there a couple of years ago when the new owner opened it to tourists, but I decided—"

"Forget it. It's all in the past. It did remind me of one thing, though. How very lucky I was to find you there."

She squeezed his fingers. Another moment elapsed.

"Your room hasn't changed, by the way," he commented lightly. "The same iron bed I made love to you on sixty-five years ago is still there."

She huffed. "Well, I hope it's not the same mattress."

He arched a bushy eyebrow. "Why?"

"One of the springs used to get me just above my left hip."

"You never said anything..."

She grinned. "It wasn't important, not when I was with you."

"I had no idea—"

"All you were interested in was my body."

"Still am. Which reminds me, Mark Priest gave me a souvenir token today. It says 'good for one trick.' How about it? For old times?"

She clucked her tongue. "I suppose you'll want a rebate, as usual."

"How about two for the price of one, instead?"

"You're a dirty old man."

"Old is relative, my dear."

She laughed, and they settled again into that companionable silence that only comes to two people at perfect peace with each other. They sat and watched the moon rise, shrinking in size as it got higher in the sky. *Everything diminishes with age,* Evvie thought. *Except love.*

"Will they make it?" Edgar finally asked.

"If she's as lucky as I have been, they will."

★ ★ ★ ★ ★

For a sneak preview of Marie Ferrarella's
DOCTOR IN THE HOUSE,
coming to NEXT *in September,*
please turn the page.

He didn't look like an unholy terror.

But maybe that reputation was exaggerated, Bailey DelMonico thought as she turned in her chair to look toward the doorway.

The man didn't seem scary at all.

Dr. Munro, or Ivan the Terrible, was tall, with an athletic build and wide shoulders. The cheekbones beneath what she estimated to be day-old stubble were prominent. His hair was light brown and just this side of unruly. Munro's hair looked as if he used his fingers for a comb and didn't care who knew it.

The eyes were brown, almost black as they were aimed at her. There was no other word for it. Aimed. As if he was debating whether or not to fire at point-blank range.

Somewhere in the back of her mind, a line from a B movie, "Be afraid—be very afraid…" whispered along the perimeter of her brain. Warning her. Almost against her will, it caused her to brace her shoulders. Bailey had to remind herself to breathe in and out like a normal person.

The chief of staff, Dr. Bennett, had tried his level best to put her at ease and had almost succeeded. But an air of tension had entered with Munro. She wondered if Dr. Bennett was bracing himself, as well, bracing for some kind of disaster or explosion.

"Ah, here he is now," Harold Bennett announced needlessly. The smile on his lips was slightly forced, and the look in his gray, kindly eyes held a warning as he looked at his chief neurosurgeon. "We were just talking about you, Dr. Munro."

"Can't imagine why," Ivan replied drily.

Harold cleared his throat, as if that would cover the less-than-friendly tone of voice Ivan had just displayed. "Dr. Munro, this is the young woman I was telling you about yesterday."

Now his eyes dissected her. Bailey felt as if she was undergoing a scalpel-less autopsy right then and there. "Ah, yes, the Stanford Special."

He made her sound like something that was listed at the top of a third-rate diner menu. There was enough contempt in his voice to offend an entire delegation from the UN.

Summoning the bravado that her parents always claimed had been infused in her since the moment she first drew breath, Bailey put out her hand. "Hello. I'm Dr. Bailey DelMonico."

Ivan made no effort to take the hand offered to him. Instead, he slid his long, lanky form bonelessly into the chair beside her. He proceeded to move the chair ever so slightly so that there was even more space between them. Ivan faced the chief of staff, but the words he spoke were addressed to her.

"You're a doctor, DelMonico, when I say you're a doctor," he informed her coldly, sparing her only one frosty glance to punctuate the end of his statement.

Harold stifled a sigh. "Dr. Munro is going to take over your education. Dr. Munro—" he fixed Ivan with a steely gaze that had been known to send lesser doctors running for their antacids, but, as always, seemed to have no effect on the chief neurosurgeon "—I want you to award her every consideration. From now on, Dr. DelMonico is to be your shadow, your sponge and your assistant." He emphasized the last word as his eyes locked with Ivan's. "Do I make myself clear?"

For his part, Ivan seemed completely unfazed. He merely nodded, his eyes and expression unreadable. "Perfectly."

His hand was on the doorknob. Bailey sprang to her feet. Her chair made a scraping noise as she moved it back and then quickly joined the neurosurgeon before he could leave the office.

Closing the door behind him, Ivan leaned over and whispered into her ear, "Just so you know, I'm going to be your worst nightmare."

Bailey DelMonico has finally
gotten her life on track, and is
passionate about her recent career
change. Nothing will stand in the way
of her becoming a doctor…that is,
until she's paired with the sharp-tongued
Dr. Ivan Munro.

Watch the sparks fly in

Doctor in the House

by *USA TODAY* Bestselling Author

Marie Ferrarella

Available September 2007

Intrigued? Read more at
TheNextNovel.com

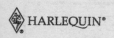

HARLEQUIN®

Mediterranean
N I G H T S™

*Sail aboard the luxurious Alexandra's Dream and
experience glamour, romance, mystery and revenge!*

Coming in October 2007...

AN AFFAIR TO
REMEMBER

by
Karen Kendall

When Captain Nikolas Pappas first fell in love with
Helena Stamos, he was a penniless deckhand and she
was the daughter of a shipping magnate. But he's
never forgiven himself for the way he left her—and
fifteen years later, he's determined to win her back.

Though the attraction is still there, Helena is hesitant
to get involved. Nick left her once...what's to stop
him from doing it again?

REQUEST YOUR FREE BOOKS!

2 FREE NOVELS PLUS 2 FREE GIFTS!

HARLEQUIN®

EVERLASTING LOVE™

Every great love has a story to tell™

YES! Please send me 2 FREE Harlequin® Everlasting Love™ novels and my 2 FREE gifts. After receiving them, if I don't wish to receive any more books, I can return the shipping statement marked "cancel." If I don't cancel, I will receive 4 brand-new novels every other month and be billed just $4.47 per book in the U.S. or $4.99 per book in Canada, plus 25¢ shipping and handling per book and applicable taxes, if any*. That's a savings of about 15% off the cover price! I understand that accepting the 2 free books and gifts places me under no obligation to buy anything. I can always return a shipment and cancel at any time. Even if I never buy another book from Harlequin, the two free books and gifts are mine to keep forever.

153 HDN ELX4   353 HDN ELYG

Name	(PLEASE PRINT)	
Address		Apt.
City	State/Prov.	Zip/Postal Code

Signature (if under 18, a parent or guardian must sign)

Mail to the **Harlequin Reader Service®:**
IN U.S.A.: P.O. Box 1867, Buffalo, NY 14240-1867
IN CANADA: P.O. Box 609, Fort Erie, Ontario L2A 5X3

Not valid to current Harlequin Everlasting Love subscribers.

Want to try two free books from another line?
Call 1-800-873-8635 or visit www.morefreebooks.com.

* Terms and prices subject to change without notice. NY residents add applicable sales tax. Canadian residents will be charged applicable provincial taxes and GST. This offer is limited to one order per household. All orders subject to approval. Credit or debit balances in a customer's account(s) may be offset by any other outstanding balance owed by or to the customer. Please allow 4 to 6 weeks for delivery.

Your Privacy: Harlequin is committed to protecting your privacy. Our Privacy Policy is available online at www.eHarlequin.com or upon request from the Reader Service. From time to time we make our lists of customers available to reputable firms who may have a product or service of interest to you. If you would prefer we not share your name and address, please check here. ☐

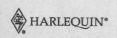

HARLEQUIN®

EVERLASTING LOVE™

Every great love has a story to tell™

An uplifting story of love and survival that spans generations.

Hayden MacNulty and Brian Conway both lived on Briar Hill Road their whole lives. As children they were destined to meet, but as a couple Hayden and Brian have much to overcome before romance ultimately flourishes.

Look for

The House on
Briar Hill Road

by award-winning author
Holly Jacobs

Available October wherever you buy books.

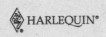

COMING NEXT MONTH

#17 THE HOUSE ON BRIAR HILL ROAD
by Holly Jacobs

A shy girl, Hayden McNulty always liked the house on Briar Hill Road, but she liked Brian Conway—the boy who lived there—even more. As children they were destined to meet, but as a couple Hayden and Brian have much to overcome before their romance ultimately flourishes. A heartfelt and uplifting story of love and survival that spans generations, and shows that true love is timeless.

Award-winning author Holly Jacobs has written more than a dozen novels for Harlequin and Silhouette Books.

#18 THE SECRET DREAMS OF EMILY PORTER
by Judith Raxten

Emily Porter finally—unexpectedly—finds the love of her life. Then Ethan Douglas dies, and she's left alone in their isolated seaside cottage. But there are signs that she may not be alone after all. Has Ethan come back to her? Will Emily be able to move on with her life…and find love again? And what does Josh Lundgren have to do with any of it?

A debut novel from an impressively talented writer. *The Secret Dreams of Emily Porter* sparkles with wit that will make you laugh—and touching moments that will bring tears to your eyes.